“Let me go and forget me— it’s the only way.”

Libby gazed out over the harbor lights. “Pia’s Italian—she’ll never agree to a divorce. And you can’t marry her with the intention of asking her to. And the baby... You can’t desert it now, how could you later? No, Keir. We can’t live on that hope, it would be wrong.” She turned impulsively.

“Let me go,” she begged, her face against his chest.

They clung together on the balcony. Then Keir, his voice ragged with emotion, muttered, “If I do that, will you stop loving me? I could bear it if I knew that somewhere you loved me.”

“I’ll always love you,” Libby whispered. “I’ll never stop now.”

Books by Nicola West

HARLEQUIN ROMANCE

2526—DEVIL'S GOLD
2592—NO ROOM IN HIS LIFE
2610—WILDTRACK
2640—THE TYZAK INHERITANCE
2646—CARVER'S BRIDE
2669—TORMENTED RHAPSODY
2718—A ROOTED SORROW

HARLEQUIN PRESENTS

589—LUCIFER'S BRAND

A Rooted Sorrow

Nicola West

Harlequin Books

TORONTO • NEW YORK • LONDON
AMSTERDAM • PARIS • SYDNEY • HAMBURG
STOCKHOLM • ATHENS • TOKYO • MILAN

Original hardcover edition published in 1984
by Mills & Boon Limited

ISBN 0-373-02718-4

Harlequin Romance first edition September 1985

Printed in U.S.A.

CHAPTER ONE

'You don't mean you're going to fly out to Malta to see Keir?' Sally Roberts sat on her bed and stared at Libby with frank disbelief in her dark eyes. 'You can't mean it. You're mad—utterly and completely mad. After the way Keir treated you two years ago you ought to be telling him to go to hell—not running to his side the moment he crooks his little finger.'

Libby snapped her suitcase shut and smiled at her flatmate. Her wide grey eyes looked even bigger than usual in their frame of sooty lashes and she flicked back her feathery black hair as she considered Sally's words. Was she mad? Should she be telling Keir to go to hell? He'd certainly hurt her badly enough two years ago, when their engagement had broken off with a snap that could have been heard round half London. But now . . . She gave herself a little shake and grinned ruefully at Sally.

'It isn't that easy,' she said. 'There are—well, complications, it's not easy to sort things out. What happened two years ago—what's happened since. I can't go into it all now. But the main thing is Keir's letter. There's something about it—it's so strange. He's in trouble of some kind and I can't make out what it is. And he says he needs me.'

Sally snorted expressively. 'Needs you! After all this time? Look, I'm sorry, Libby, but can't you accept what happened? See him for what he is? All right, he may need you, but do you need him? Or is this going to stir up a whole hornet's nest of misery just when you were rebuilding your life so well?'

Libby shrugged and lifted the suitcase to the floor.

'That's something we'll just have to work out,' she said quietly. 'And the only way we can do that is for me to do what he asks—go out there. I can't just ignore his letter, Sally. It—it's like a cry for help.'

Sally snorted again. 'And what about Terry?' she asked. 'Or doesn't he count any more?'

Libby bit her soft lip. With a guilty pang she realised that she hadn't thought about Terry since Keir's letter had arrived. She wasn't being fair at all to the pleasant young man who had been her constant escort for the past six months.

'Yes, I'm sorry about Terry,' she admitted. 'But you know there's never been any commitment between us. We've had a lot of fun—but that's all it's been.'

'As far as you're concerned, perhaps,' Sally said shortly. 'I'm not so sure about Terry. I've seen the way he looks at you sometimes. Still—' she shrugged '—I suppose it's your affair. Keir's obviously still got some kind of hold over you. I just hope you don't find yourself in a situation you can't handle.'

'Oh, I don't think that'll happen,' Libby answered lightly. 'After all, we *were* engaged—I know him pretty well.' But she turned away so that Sally would not see the crease of anxiety on her smooth brow. How well, after all, *had* she known Keir? How well did she know him now, after two years apart? He must have changed in that time—she was sure she had. Would she find him the Keir she had known—and loved? Or would he be different—a stranger, his blue eyes cold as they had been the last time she had seen him? And just why, after all this time, did he want to see her again? Why had he sent that strange letter, half arrogant, half pleading?

And why, she wondered ruefully, was she dropping everything—her job, her social life—to fly to his side? As if, as Sally had perceptively remarked, he still had some strange hold over her?

That was just it, she thought as she stared out at the grey London street below the flat. He *did* have some kind of hold over her. And that was why she was going to Malta to meet him again. To find out just what that hold was—and to find out how, or even if, it could be broken.

The aircraft was filled with cheerful families and couples, all evidently bound for Malta on holiday. Behind Libby was a small child who peppered his parents with questions for the first half of the journey and then fell suddenly asleep, to the relief of everyone around. Libby looked out of the window and then read the free magazine she had found in the seat pocket. Printed in the style of a newspaper, it was full of items about Malta—where to go, what to see, what to eat and drink. Very useful if you were going on holiday, she thought, but that wasn't the purpose of her journey. She would probably see very little of the island, and that seemed a pity when she realised how interesting it must be, with its long and varied history. Perhaps another time—when her mind was free to relax . . .

The aircraft flew steadily down the coast of Italy and past Sicily, with a view of the smoke of Mount Etna, before leaving land behind for the last stretch over the Mediterranean before Malta. A stir of excitement rustled through the plane as passengers craned their necks for a first glimpse of the island. In spite of her preoccupation, Libby felt her own excitement rise as she caught sight of the jagged shape, almost blindingly white in the hot sun, a rocky fortress in the blue sea with its attendant islands of Gozo and Comino like stones thrown from the shore. She peered down, fascinated by the starkness of the place—there were only a few clusters of trees here and there and, as far as she could see, no grassy areas at all. Yet, as the plane swept lower, she could see a blaze of colours—a large garden, perhaps a public park, she guessed. And there were huge cavities, too, that must be quarries, where the stone to build all the houses was gouged out. Her final glimpse before the plane dropped too low to see any more was of a harbour, filled with coloured boats tossing on the white-flecked ripples.

The plane touched down and taxied to the end of the runway before turning back. The atmosphere now was electric with excitement as holidaymakers gathered their hand luggage together. Libby stared out at the white buildings and felt suddenly panic-stricken. What had she been doing, getting excited about Malta? In a short time now she would be meeting Keir again, and she realised suddenly that she had no idea at all how to greet him. They had parted in anger and bitterness and had had no contact between then and the arrival of his letter just a few days ago. In an effort to remind herself of why she had come, she pulled the envelope from her pocket. It was crumpled from having been opened and read so frequently since she had received it, and she knew it almost by heart, but she stared at it now as if she had never seen it before, her brain registering only a few words here and there—words that leapt out at her, burning themselves into her mind.

'Libby, my love . . . I've been missing you so much . . . we've been apart too long . . . can't you come to me? Come now, my sweet, and let's make up for lost time . . . I need you . . . I need you . . .'

There was more, but Libby still could not understand some of the things he had written. It was all so vague—hints at some kind of trouble, references to events she had never heard of. And, more clearly, reminders of their own past, when it had been happy, before bitterness broke in. Reminders that had brought a lump to her throat and tears to her eyes; reminders that even now brought her memories sharply into her mind. And through it all, that strange, indefinable sense of urgency; that bond that still held between her and the man she had once been engaged to.

The other passengers were standing up now, crowding the gangways, eager to get off and start their holiday. Libby watched them and decided to stay in her seat until the last. There was little point in adding to the crowd and she certainly wouldn't get off any faster—she wasn't even sure now that she wanted to. In fact, if anyone had offered her the chance of staying on the plane and going straight back to London, she would have taken it! But nobody suggested such a thing and she sat there, staring unseeingly out of the window and letting her mind drift back, as it had so many times before, to that magical summer when she had first met Keir.

She had been just twenty-two, a year out of university and working as a sub-editor on a women's fashion magazine. The world had been her oyster; behind her was her life in Devon with her parents and sister Claire, before her was all the excitement of working in London, meeting people she had only read about or seen on TV and never dreamed she might actually talk to one day. Even now, as a humble sub-editor, she hadn't met many, but at the parties given by the magazine she had talked to some of the celebrities who had been interviewed for the features page. And it was at one of these parties that she had met Keir Salinger.

Keir, at thirty-three, was already well-known as a novelist and biographer. He had published his first novel when no older than Libby herself, and gone on from strength to strength, winning several major prizes and becoming a TV personality on the major chat-shows. He was also in some considerable danger of becoming a sex-symbol too, with his tall, rangy figure, his burnished gold hair and deep blue eyes. The mobile mouth could smile with a charm that had a good many women turning their TVs on whenever he was due to appear, more for the pleasure of gazing at him than to listen to what he had to say. And it was becoming equally well-known that this was a facet of fame that didn't appeal much to Keir Salinger.

So Libby had been slightly surprised to see him at the party at all. Lately, she had heard, Keir Salinger had been turning into something of a recluse, refusing to appear on TV unless it was for a definite discussion and even threatening to sue one or two newspapers which had published stories about him and the many ladies he could be seen around London with.

Libby had been nervous of meeting him—not that she would be likely to anyway, she told herself as she dressed for the party. He would have more important people to talk to than a mere sub-editor. So when she had found herself handing him a drink, she had turned away immediately.

'Hey, wait a minute!' A long arm stretched out to bar her way, and sensitive fingers caught her sleeve. 'You're not going to leave me all on my own, are you?'

Libby turned back and looked uncertainly at him. 'But you can't be on your own, Mr Salinger—there must be heaps of people here who want to talk to you.'

'Oh yes, I'm sure,' he grimaced. 'But not so many *I* want to talk to. You don't have to rush off, do you? You're not employed to hand drinks around?'

'No—I work on the magazine.' Libby looked at him again, still feeling hesitant. He couldn't seriously want to talk to her. 'Have you met our editor? She's just over—'

'Yes, I've met your editor, your features editor, your beauty editor, your fashion editor and your pictures editor,' he told her forcibly, 'and to my way of thinking that's enough editors for any man. Now I want to talk to *you*. Just what do you do on the magazine?'

Libby dimpled at him, unable to resist her reply. 'I'm a sub-editor, Mr Salinger. Want to change your mind?' And she laughed as he clapped his hand to his forehead in mock despair.

'Obviously there's no escape,' he declared. 'You must be breeding. All right, I give in—I'll talk to the sub-editor. But not about editing, if you don't mind. And not about me. Tell me about yourself.'

'Me?' Libby's uncertainty returned. Was he mocking her? 'But I'm not interesting at all, Mr Salinger, I—'

'Well, I'll be the judge of that,' he returned easily. 'And let's cut out the "Mr", shall we? Keir's the name, as you very well know. And you're—?'

'Libby. But honestly, Mr—Keir—there *isn't* anything interesting about me. I've only been working here a year and—'

'And before that?'

'I was at university. Nothing very grand—a redbrick—'

'Where?' His questions were rapping out now and Libby would have felt resentful if he hadn't been smiling at her in that devastating way. A tiny warning sounded somewhere in her mind, a warning of danger, but she dismissed it. What possible danger could Keir Salinger be to her? He was just passing time at a party, that was all.

'Exeter,' she said, answering his question. 'My family live in Devon—near Dartmoor. My father's a doctor.'

He nodded and she wondered if he was losing interest. Not that she would blame him if he was—she *had* told him that she had nothing to talk about. But she couldn't help feeling a little disappointed, even so, at the way his eyes were now roving over the rest of the room.

Suddenly he seemed to come to a decision. The bright blue eyes returned to her face with an almost physical shock and he reached out and laid a hand on her arm, sending a tingle through her whole body.

'You're *not* going to leave me on my own, are you?' he said persuasively. 'People are beginning to leave. And if I stay here much longer your revered editor is going to bear down on me again and I'll feel obliged to take her out to dinner. And I'd much rather take you.' The smile warmed his face again and Libby stared at him, bemused. She couldn't be hearing right. Had he really just asked her to have dinner with him? Feeling her cheeks flush scarlet, she began to stammer something, but he cut her short.

'Get your coat or whatever you've got, Libby,' he murmured, and the deepness of his voice sent a thrill down her spine. 'Let's get away from here to some place where we can talk properly. I've got a feeling we're going to have a lot to say to each other.'

In a dream, Libby fetched her coat and returned to find him waiting by the door. Someone else was talking to him now, but as soon as Keir caught Libby's eye he excused himself and came across to her. His hand was warm under her elbow as he guided her out of the tall building and led her across to a grey, low-slung Porsche waiting at the opposite kerb.

Libby got in, still in a daze. She just couldn't begin to understand why this man, rich and famous, attractive enough to be taking out the most sought-after girls in London, should want to share his evening with her. They hadn't even talked for more than a few moments, and nothing she had said was intelligent or witty enough to have caught his attention. Perhaps, she thought wryly, he was just tired of beautiful and intelligent women and felt like relaxing with someone a little less demanding. There surely could be no other reason.

He took her to a small French restaurant where he was obviously well-known, and they were shown to a corner table surrounded by tall green pot plants. It was like a private bower, Libby thought, and her bewilderment grew. Then, as she handed over her coat and slipped into the chair, she shook herself mentally. What did it matter why he had brought her here? The best thing to do was simply enjoy it—because if one thing was certain, it was that there would never be a second occasion like this. Keir Salinger would have had enough of ingenuous unsophistication by the end of the evening and be glad to return to his more usual kind of girl-friend.

And having thought that, Libby did relax and enjoy herself, although she could never remember the evening in detail afterwards. It was all a warm blur of delicious food and drink, laughter and an increasingly incredulous feeling that somehow she had known and been waiting for Keir all her life. And when she slipped once more into the passenger seat of the Porsche, she was conscious of a deep regret that it was to be a once-in-a-lifetime experience.

But it hadn't been, after all. Keir hadn't spoken much as he drove her back to the flat she shared with three other girls, and she had expected him to wish her a brief goodnight before driving away, out of her life. He had been so silent, in fact, that she'd begun to come out of her golden dream and wonder uneasily if she had offended him in some way. And then, as the Porsche came to a smooth halt, he had turned to her and slipped a strong arm round her shoulders.

'That was just what I needed, Libby,' he told her in his deep, quiet voice. 'An evening entirely without pretensions. I was beginning to wonder if there were any girls like you left.'

'Girls like me?' Libby repeated uncertainly, and he nodded, drawing her a fraction closer.

'That's what I said. Girls who still look at the world as if it's something good—something fresh and new and full of surprises. There's nothing cynical about you, Libby. You can still enjoy the simple things, and that's something that's been missing from my life lately.'

Libby gazed at him, still not quite sure what he meant. Even now, she thought, he might be sending me up, but somehow she didn't think he was.

Keir spoke again. 'Let's not look too deeply into things, Libby. Let's just enjoy ourselves. What about a day in the country at the weekend? A picnic, a walk, something like that. Appeal to you?'

'Oh, *yes*,' Libby breathed, and he laughed.

'That's settled then. I'll call for you at—well, let's make an early start—say nine-thirty on Sunday. Don't bother to do anything—I'll bring everything we need—you just bring yourself, all right?'

'All right,' Libby agreed, still bemused, and he smiled and then drew her close and placed his lips firmly on hers.

Libby was shaking as she got out of the car and went into the house. She had been kissed before, of course—Libby had never been short of boy-friends at university, though she hadn't had any serious relationships since coming to London—but nothing had prepared her for the weakness that had invaded her when Keir Salinger kissed her. She touched her lips gently, still feeling the firm, cool pressure of his, remembering the way they had moved over hers, sending a flame of desire through her, making her cling to him with a sudden desperation. Keir had held her close, his hands stroking her body with a tenderness that she had never experienced before; then, with a final gentle kiss, he had released her and sat looking at her, his eyes dark.

'Go on, Libby,' he said gently. 'Time you were in bed. I'll see you on Sunday.' And he swung his long legs out of the car, came round and opened Libby's door and guided her gently up the steps.

That had been the beginning. The rest of that summer had been as golden as Libby's dream—a long kaleidoscope of days in the country, or by the sea, evenings at the theatre or concerts, or just walking through the parks; rainy days spent indoors listening to music and one hot night when a tremendous thunderstorm had broken and they had watched it together from the window of Keir's flat.

That had been the evening Libby had tried hardest to forget during the past two years, but now as she sat waiting to get off the plane in Malta, she allowed it to come back to her mind. It was the night Keir had proposed to her; the night they had become engaged.

Libby had never been afraid of thunder, but that storm had been particularly fierce, the crack of noise directly overhead and almost simultaneous with the searing flash of light, and she had been glad of Keir's arms around her. Shivering, she had snuggled closer, revelling in the hardness of his body, the warmth and musky male scent of him; and then, as he held her, she had become aware of a change in him, a different kind of tension in the way he held her. She turned her face up to his, expecting him to kiss her, and found his eyes on hers, dark with an emotion she couldn't quite fathom, but which sent a thrill trembling through her limbs.

'Keir?' she whispered, and then he did kiss her, a kiss

that told her just how much and how badly he wanted more, a kiss that made her want more too. She clung to him, her body shaking with the thunder that shook the air, and felt him lift her in his arms and carry her over to the sofa. He laid her down and she looked up at him with wide eyes. And then he shook his head, and drew back from her.

'No,' he muttered, 'this isn't right, this isn't the way it has to be. Not with you, Libby—never with you.'

A stab of fear pierced Libby and she raised herself up to look at him. 'What do you mean, Keir? What are you saying? What's wrong?'

'Wrong?' he said. 'Nothing's wrong, Libby, my sweet—only me. I've just realised—realised what I was doing.' He sat on the sofa beside her, holding her palm against his cheek. 'From the beginning, I knew you were different. That was what attracted me—your freshness, your total lack of cynicism and world-weariness. You were so different—and that's the way I wanted you to stay.' He paused. 'We've had some very sweet months together, Libby. It's been like regaining my own youth, sharing yours. But I'm not a callow boy. I'm a man—I've been around. I need a bit more than innocent friendship.'

'And don't you think I do, too?' Libby whispered. 'I'm not a child, Keir—I'm a woman. And I've become even more so since we've been together. Whatever it is you want—don't you think I want it just as much?'

Keir looked soberly down at her. 'Oh yes, I know you want it just as badly as I do,' he said. 'But it's not going to be that way, Libby. For you, this would be a first time—am I right?' He watched her nod. 'That's something you'll never have again and it's something you shouldn't throw away. Because you're not one of those women who can take sex lightly. I've got to know you pretty well over the past few months, Libby, and I know that for you it would be serious—a commitment.'

In her heart, Libby knew this was true. But she knew, too, that she was already committed to Keir, finally and irrevocably; that whether he loved her or not she belonged to him. She had no hope that their relationship would continue; Keir would tire of her, find someone else, and she would have to make her life without him. So couldn't she have as much as possible to remember? Couldn't she know that he had loved her, for at least a little while?

'Don't worry about that, Keir,' she whispered. 'I want you to love me—even if it's only for tonight.' But he shook his head again and her heart sank.

'I told you, Libby, it can't be like that. You deserve better. You deserve a man who will love you and cherish you—a man who will marry you.'

Libby felt her body turn cold. She stared up at him, her eyes huge with appeal. What was he telling her? That this was goodbye?

'Keir,' she begged, 'don't say that. I don't want anyone else—only you. I won't be a nuisance to you, Keir, I won't make demands, I—' The rest of her words were lost as Kcir caught hcr up against him, prcssing hcr facc against his broad chest, his hands in her hair, his voice muttering incoherently in her ear.

'Libby, don't,' she heard at last. 'My God, what have you been thinking? I never meant to make you talk like that—I was trying to tell you . . . Oh God, I'm making a mess of this. But I've never—I've never proposed to anyone before.' His voice shook with a sudden laugh. 'Will you believe that? I thought I'd been around—thought I was a man of the world—and I don't even know how to propose . . . how to ask the girl I love to become my wife!'

Libby removed her face from his chest and stared at him. 'Your *wife*? But I thought—I thought you were—'

'Trying to finish it?' Keir shook his head. 'Never. You're an essential part of my life now, Libby. I can't do without you. We belong together. And that's why I'm not going to do anything to hurt you. I'm not even going to make love to you—not until we're married. You're going to go to the altar in white, Libby, if that's what you want, and know that you have every right to do so.'

They had spent the rest of that evening making plans, the thunderstorm forgotten. The wedding was to be as soon as possible, but as Libby wanted to be married in her own home village on the edge of Dartmoor, their first task was to go to see her parents and make the arrangements. Keir was willing to go along with whatever Libby wanted—to marry her, he said, he was prepared to pass any test, including a big society wedding if she wanted one. To which Libby replied that if she had been the kind of girl to want a big society wedding, he wouldn't have been waiting to marry her anyway.

'True,' Keir acknowledged with a grin. 'But it will be quite terrifying enough for me to meet your parents anyway, had you thought of that? They might not approve of your marrying an older man.'

'They'll approve of any man so long as I love him and he loves me,' Libby answered confidently. 'Shall we go down this weekend? I'll ring and arrange it, and we can see the vicar, too, and fix a date.'

'Madam, I am entirely in your hands,' Keir said with mock gravity, and then his expression changed and he pulled her to him and kissed her with sudden passion. 'Just get it fixed as soon as possible, will you?' he ground out against her lips. 'I'm not used to restraining myself like this—I can't promise how long it will last . . .'

Libby's confidence in her family's reception of Keir had been wholly justified. Her father, older and wearier than when she had last seen him, had thoroughly approved of Keir's positive attitude to life, and had seen in his strength something that Libby needed to balance her own more mercurial character. Her mother, less ready to take to strangers on sight, had very quickly given Keir her trust and had told Libby privately that she had been very lucky indeed to find such a man. She had almost, indeed, given her daughter the impression that she was surprised by Keir's choice, but Libby knew her mother rather well and smiled at her words, feeling thankful only that Keir had been made so welcome and clearly met with her parents' approval.

As for Libby's elder sister Claire, Keir could do no wrong. In fact, Claire remarked as the two girls walked round the garden together after supper while Keir talked with their father, if she hadn't been already happily married and expecting her first child within the next few weeks, she might well have been ragingly jealous.

'Don't worry, I'm not,' she added reassuringly. 'Simon and I are very happy and I wouldn't swop him for anyone on earth. But if he hadn't been around—well . . . Your Keir is a very attractive man, Libby.'

'I know. I still can't believe my luck.' Libby lifted her face to the evening air and looked at the blue line of the moors beyond the garden. 'But what about you, Claire? Is it true what Mum was hinting at—that you're having twins? But that's fantastic! Are you pleased?'

'Half thrilled and half terrified!' Claire admitted. 'It'll be fun—so long as I can cope. That's the part that terrifies me. But Simon will help a lot and at least I've got Mum and Dad, and plenty of friends around here.' She glanced at Libby. 'What about you—where are you going to live when you're married? Are you going to give up work?'

'Probably. I'll have to really—Keir's work takes him to so many different places. So I'll live wherever he is. I can help him with his work, anyway—editing, proof-reading, that kind of thing. We haven't really thought about it much.'

'Oh my, you really are in a dream, aren't you,' Claire teased. 'Well, I hope it all works out for you both. And I'm sure it will. I never saw a couple more in love—not after me and Simon, at least.'

'It'll work out,' Libby said confidently. 'Nothing can come between Keir and me—nothing.'

And that was what she had believed, both then and during the following weeks of their engagement, longer than they had intended because Claire had begged them to wait until her twins were born and she could, as she put it, appear in the wedding photographs without taking up space for half a dozen other guests.

Which just went to show, she thought ruefully as the last few passengers disappeared along the gangway, that you could never be absolutely certain of anything. Because something had come between herself and Keir—something totally unexpected and unforeseen. And it had broken them apart, leaving their precious, golden love a smatter of fragments too tiny and too fragile ever to piece together again.

Or were they? Was Keir's call for her his own acknowledgment that their love had, after all, survived? Was he, in the next few minutes, going to take her in his arms and tell her that it had all been a ghastly mistake, that he loved her and needed her and couldn't let her go?

And if he did—what was her own reaction going to be? Just what did she feel about Keir Salinger now, after the impact he had had on her life, the hurt he had dealt her and the way he had left her?

That, she thought grimly, was what she had come to Malta to find out. And she wouldn't find out by sitting here and going over it all again. She had to move—get up, gather her luggage together, walk out of this plane and into the airport buildings where Keir would be waiting. She had to face him—and whatever the future held.

CHAPTER TWO

THE Customs officers were waiting impatiently as Libby came through the control with her luggage, well after everyone else had dispersed. She walked across the wide space, its floor covered with cool tiles, and looked doubtfully out at the sunshine. Somewhere out there Keir was waiting for her. She hesitated, her doubts flowing back, but it was too late now. She had burned her boats—if you could say that about someone who had just flown in, she thought ruefully. There was only one way to go and that was forward.

Taking a deep breath, she picked up her cases and walked out through the glass doors into the warmth of the October air. At something over seventy degrees, it was like entering a warm bath after the cool, drizzly day she had left behind in England and, anxious though she was, she couldn't help stopping for a moment just to savour the feel of sunshine on her skin. But her moment wasn't to last for long, because before she opened her eyes again a shadow had fallen across her face and a deep voice, heart-shakingly familiar, was saying her name.

'Libby? Libby, is it really you?'

Libby's eyes flew open as, with a gasp, she took an involuntary step back. Keir! Even though she had known he would be meeting her, even though she had known this moment would come, she still couldn't help the shock that ran through her entire body. Her mind reeled and she lifted a hand to her face, staring up at him. As she swayed, he put out a hand to steady her, and she felt the familiar tingle run from his fingers up the length of her arm.

'Don't look like that, Libby,' he said quietly. 'I know it's been a long time—too long. But don't look as if—as if I'd come back from the dead.'

But that's just how it is, Libby wanted to cry out. That's exactly how it is. Her gaze moved over him, taking in every detail. The broad shoulders, the narrow waist and hips; the corn-gold hair, the deep blue eyes that could look as dark as the twilit sea when he was moved, or as pale as a winter sky when he was angry. The lips that could, with the merest touch, destroy every shred of will-power in Libby's mind.

This was how she remembered him, this was the Keir she had fallen in love with and planned to marry. So what had happened to that other Kier—the one who had looked at her with cold eyes, the one who had walked out of her life? What had happened to change things?

He drew her close and kissed her, but for once Libby could not respond. Her mind was too full of doubts and she knew that there were too many questions to be answered before they could regain their old relationship. As his lips left hers, she caught an odd expression in his eyes; partly hurt, partly quizzical. But he said nothing, merely bent to lift her cases and jerked his head towards the car park.

'The car's over here.' Without another glance he led the way across to the open-topped coupé, and Libby followed, feeling indefinably chastened. It was as if he had tested her and found her wanting.

A small seed of anger germinated in her as she thought that. She hadn't come all this way to pass exams, for goodness' sake! What right did he have to find fault with her, after all this time? Was she supposed to fall into his arms without so much as a word of explanation? Well, if that was what he expected he was doomed to disappointment, and the sooner he realised it, the better. He wasn't the only one to have changed in the past two years. There had been a few changes in Libby, too—like the fact that she was a lot more confident now, a lot more able to take care of herself.

At least, that was what she hoped. But in spite of all her doubts, Libby was already uncomfortably aware of Keir's magnetism. And she remembered what Sally had said that afternoon in the flat—was it really only yesterday?

Keir Salinger's got some kind of hold over you, Sally had told her. And Libby had known even then that it was true.

Keir held the door open for Libby to slide into the passenger seat and as she came close to him she raised her eyes to meet his. He was looking at her in the same odd way—shuttered, but with a shadow of pain behind his eyes. And Libby felt even more bewildered. She didn't know what it was she had expected from this meeting—passion, reconciliation, perhaps even hostility. Whatever it was, she hadn't expected this enigmatic look of hurt—as if Keir himself were searching for something that wasn't there.

Perhaps she was imagining it all, she thought bleakly as she settled herself and waited for Keir to stow away her luggage. Perhaps he was simply regretting ever having asked her to come. Perhaps, even now, behind that gaunt profile—thinner, surely, than she remembered it—he was wondering how soon it would be before she went back.

They were away from the airfield now, driving along white roads that were bordered by rough stone-built walls, reinforced in places with oil drums. Libby looked out of the window curiously. Tiny brown fields, each one separated from the others by rubble walls—which must in themselves have taken up quite a lot of room—and, as they approached the town, what seemed to be a cross between a demolition site and a half-finished estate. There were houses that were completed, pleasant, modern homes, standing next to a mess of walling that was still being worked on, while some of it seemed to have been abandoned altogether, and a few of the half-finished houses were apparently occupied already.

Somewhere in her memory Libby remembered hearing that Malta had suffered badly in the war. Hadn't she seen an old film about it on TV once? Perhaps they were still recovering—perhaps, since the British Navy had moved out, Malta was having a struggle to keep going. Or perhaps they just worked in a different way here and she was applying the wrong standard to what was, after all, a foreign country.

One forgot that it was foreign, though, when there were so many signs of British occupation—signposts that could have come from an English country lane, the elderly British cars that were evidenly left behind by their owners several years before. But there was little vegetation to remind you of Britain, though—Malta was, as Libby had been told before, little more than a rock with only a few patches of fertile ground.

'Where are we going?' she asked after a few moments, when it seemed clear that Keir wasn't going to speak first.

'I'm taking you to my flat,' he said briefly. 'I don't live in Valletta—I've got a place outside, in a village called Zurrieq. It's quieter—so long as you aren't on the road to the factory—and not far from the coast.' He glanced sideways at her. 'I'm sorry, I didn't ask if you had a good flight.'

'Yes, it was fine, thank you,' Libby said. Oh, what had

happened? Why did they have to talk to each other in this stilted manner? 'Keir, why did you—' she began impulsively, but he cut her short.

'Let's talk later, Libby. The standard of driving isn't all it might be here—I have to watch the road.' His mouth closed firmly, ending the conversation, and Libby fell silent again, feeling snubbed. It was true that the Maltese drove their cars with a careless abandon that accounted for many of the dents on them, but she wasn't convinced that Keir was incapable of driving and talking at the same time. He never had been before.

It wasn't far to Zurrieq, and not far enough to Libby's mind. She was beginning to wish heartily that she had never come and was dreading the moment when they did begin to talk. Though what Keir wanted to talk about, she couldn't begin to imagine. Apart from that first moment at the airport when he had looked at her with hunger in his eyes, he didn't seem a bit pleased to see her. And there was definitely something not quite right about him—something she had never sensed before and couldn't put a name to now, but something that filled her with an uneasy presentiment of danger.

Libby chided herself. What possible kind of danger could there be? Keir had never been a violent man—had he?—and the biggest threat to her had always been his exceptional and sensual virility, which had almost swamped her more than once. And even that wasn't quite fair, she admitted honestly, because on those wild and almost frightening occasions, it had been Keir who drew back, while Libby's body had cried out for more.

They were coming now into a large village, a maze of twisting streets and half-built houses. It seemed that there was a large programme of reconstruction going on in Malta, and from the look of the houses already completed it was going to make the island very attractive indeed. Libby watched with interest as Keir drove the car expertly through streets that were little more than alley-ways and pulled up in front of a large square building that was evidently an apartment block, with balconies outside each large picture window.

'Welcome to Jasmine,' he said ironically, getting out of the car and swinging her luggage off the back seat.

'Jasmine? Is that the name of the house?'

'That's right. The Maltese are very fond of flower names for their homes. Or perhaps I should say flowery.' For a moment the old familiar smile crinkled at her. 'The place next door is called Fairyland!' Then his expression resumed its dourness. 'Let's get inside.'

Libby followed him through the door and across a tiled hall, decorated with potted plants that would have turned an English florist green with envy. Swiss cheeses and castor oil plants reached to the high ceiling, while others she couldn't name stood in troughs. The effect was cool and exotic, enhanced by the view through the picture window of a deep valley running down to the sea.

'You can see the same thing better from my window,' Keir told her brusquely, and she followed him into a lift which took them up three floors. Libby couldn't repress a gasp of pure delight as she went into the big sitting-room of the flat. As Keir had promised, the view was even better from here; she could see tiny coloured boats on the stretch of dancing blue water, and the valley was green, filled with small trees and bushes. There didn't seem to be any river in it—she remembered dimly that there were none on Malta—but presumably it filled with water when the rain came and so was just fertile enough to sustain a particularly tough kind of plant life.

'How long have you lived here?' she asked, looking round at the spacious room. 'Are you just on holiday?'

She glanced at Keir and caught him watching her with that strange, enigmatic expression again. Flushing uncomfortably, she hurried on: 'I'm afraid I haven't kept up much with what you've been doing.'

Immediately it was as if a shutter had come down over his face, yet what else could she have said? It was true, wasn't it? Did he expect her to have kept a scrap-book on his affairs, or something?'

Not that it wouldn't have been easy. Keir Salinger had been easy meat for the gossip columnists until he had virtually retired from the limelight a year or so ago. There had been no lack of girls in his life. Most of them had been merely transitory, just taken out once or twice. But there had been one or two who had lasted longer. The beautiful Italian countess for example—Pia, wasn't that her name? What had happened to her?

'No, I'm not on holiday,' Keir said harshly. 'I'm working—writing a history of Malta. It's a long job—there's quite a lot of history to write about—and I've been here for three months so far.'

'It must be quite a big job,' Libby said politely. Once again they seemed to be trapped in this glass cage—or, rather, two glass cages with no way from one to the other. How could she reach Keir? Did she even want to? But if she didn't, there would be no point in her journey at all. And there must be some point—Keir never did anything without good reason.

'It is.' He didn't seem to want to talk about his work, so Libby said no more. She was tired of trying to break through anyway. Hadn't she done enough in simply dropping everything and flying out here to be with him? Perhaps he regretted the letter he had written her. The letter that had called her his sweet and begged her to make up for lost time . . .

Keir turned abruptly. 'You must be needing a drink,'

he said. 'What'll it be? Martini, gin, or—' his lip curled faintly '—perhaps a nice cup of tea. Isn't that what English people always want the moment they set foot on foreign soil? Only I warn you, the water here has an odd effect on tea. It's desalinated and seems to do something to the flavour.'

'I'd like a cup of coffee, please,' Libby said steadily, and his glance flickered over her for a moment before he nodded and went through a door to the kitchen. Libby didn't follow him. She wandered over to the big window and stood looking out. The apartment was built at the head of the green valley and this room was evidently at the back of it. The kitchen would look over the road where Keir had parked the car. She noticed a long building on one side of the steep valley, and a road twining along the edge of the other. Cars passed along it, but they were too far away to make any sound.

She wondered where Keir intended that she should stay. Here in his flat? She wasn't sure she liked that idea—not while there was still this glass wall between them. And even when—if—it was demolished; what then? Would they really be on their old footing, as the letter had suggested? Or would the quarrel that had split them apart prove too strong for any love that there might be left?

Keir came through from the kitchen carrying a tray of coffee, which he set down on a low table in front of the window. He sat down in the chair opposite Libby and gave her a quick glance from under hooded lids. It was almost as if he were nervous of *her*, Libby thought in sudden astonishment. As if he were just as uncertain in this odd situation—as if he, too, were wondering what to say next.

Well, they couldn't go on like this! *Someone* had to make a start. Libby took a deep breath.

'Why did you ask me to come here, Keir? What is it you want? I—' But again he cut her short.

'Don't let's talk about that now, Libby. Let's just get to know each other again, shall we?' Again that strange look in his eyes. 'Let's talk about old times—the fun we had. Remember? Remember the day we went walking on Dartmoor, that first time I came down to see your family? We saw a foal being born to a wild pony, remember that? It was magic. And the day we went to Salcombe and hired a sailing dinghy. You'd never told me you could sail and we said next time we'd have one each and have races. Only we never did, did we? We couldn't bear to be even that much apart.'

Libby's eyes misted with tears. What was he doing, bringing back these memories that were so sweet—and so painfully bitter? She had tried so hard to forget, knowing that the memory of such happiness could only make her loss more unbearable? Didn't he realise that by forcing her to remember he was practising what could only amount to refined torture?

'Keir . . .' she murmured, but he was oblivious to her voice and her pleading eyes, staring out of the huge window down the valley, his gaze remote on the sparkling waves and the dancing boats. Didn't he understand—or didn't he care?

Or maybe it was something else. Maybe he understood all too well. Maybe the letter he had sent, this nostalgic return to the past, were both part of some sinister scheme for revenge. Could that really be it? Could Keir be that sadistic? Had she hurt him as badly as he had hurt her—so that two years later, when she had begun to rebuild her life, he could deliberately seek her out and open up all the old wounds, hurt her all over again?

It was a fantastic idea, surely too fantastic, but wouldn't it account for the strangeness she had sensed in him? Wouldn't it explain that odd, enigmatic expression she'd caught in his eyes and on his lean, brown face? The tautness round his eyes—the tension that kept his whole body as tightly wound as a spring?

Questions, questions, Libby thought wearily. She was sick of them, sick of not knowing, of wondering . . . Why couldn't everything be straightforward, cut and dried? Why did it all have to be so *complicated*? That time Keir was remembering as he stared out to sea with that hooded gaze—it hadn't been complicated then. It had all seemed so beautifully simple; an easy matter of loving and living, with no doubts or uncertainties. Hadn't that been the way things ought to be? Or had it been some cruel joke?

'It was like being back in a golden childhood, with all the advantages of being adult,' Keir was saying softly. 'We put care and responsibility behind us for those few weeks, didn't we, Libby? We sailed and swam and rode and walked, and never gave a thought to what came next. And why should we? Everyone deserves a holiday from the world at some time in their lives, and what better time than when we fall in love? But it has to end, doesn't it? We have to come back—face reality. We have to be able to cope when things go wrong.' He paused and his gaze came back to rest on Libby's face, shocking her with the dark pain that lurked behind his eyes. 'What went wrong for us, Libby?' he murmured. 'What was our reality?'

Libby couldn't speak. She sat staring at him, almost mesmerised by that magnetic gaze, shaken by the torture that she sensed in the taut body. There was something here she couldn't begin to understand . . . But why was he asking this? How *could* he ask her what had gone wrong between them? How could he be so insensitive? He had known—surely he had known!

Before she could speak, Keir's expression changed again, the pain wiped from his eyes to leave them curiously blank before he leapt to his feet. 'I'm sorry, Libby—forget it. I'm being morbid, and on the first day of your holiday, too! Now—what would you like to do? I thought we'd eat in Valletta tonight, there are one or two rather good restaurants there, and perhaps you'd like to look around the town first. It really comes to life in the early evening, after the siesta—all the shops open and it seems as if the whole of Malta comes to gossip!' He stood over her, big and broad, the sun glinting through the window on his burnished hair. 'Why don't you go along and have a shower and change, and then we'll go? Nothing elaborate—just a pretty dress or skirt, whatever you like.'

Libby followed him through the flat in a daze. His mood changed so quickly, she couldn't keep up with him. And that wasn't the Keir she remembered—she had always been the volatile one. And why had he talked as if she were here on holiday? Was he indeed regretting having sent for her? Or had she been right in thinking about revenge—was this another subtle part of that?

Well, she would find out sooner or later. Things couldn't go on like this, there would have to be a show-down, but she wasn't at all sure she could cope with it tonight. Tonight! She stood in the bedroom Keir had shown her to and looked round at the cool walls, the light cane furniture, the big, white-covered bed that stood near the shuttered windows. Was she being foolish to stay here, alone with Keir and especially Keir in this strange mood? But she couldn't face the idea of going to find somewhere else. Going out for a meal was just about all she could manage tonight.

Valletta was all that Keir had promised, and more. He parked the car near the centre and they walked across a big square, lined with shops selling all manner of goods—Libby had never seen such a selection in a small city before. Keir didn't seem to be in any hurry and his tension had relaxed a little as they wandered through the arcades, looking in the windows at the array of Maltese crafts—golden-brown pottery, delicate filigree silver jewellery, mysterious blue glass and exquisite lace. Malta could claim expertise in all these crafts, Keir told her, and you could see them all in action; many of them in the villages where women sat at their cottage doors making the lace with traditional skill or potters worked in small sheds. Or all together in the craft village just outside Rabat, a collection of buildings on a disused airfield that housed the Mdina glassworks as well as a host of other craftworks.

The shopping area was all new, recently built, but as soon as they passed out of it the scene changed dramatically and Libby found herself staring in amazement at the ruined pillars of the old Opera House. The older part of the city lay on its far side and Keir led her round it, pausing to let her take in the devastation.

'A relic of the war,' he said briefly. 'All this part was bombed heavily over several months—it's a wonder there was any left. As you can see, there's been a lot of rebuilding and expansion, but this has been left deliberately, so that people will remember.'

'I think I would want to forget,' Libby said slowly, staring at the desolation of the ruins. 'After all, that happened a long time ago now—a generation ago. It doesn't do any good to keep hatred alive—to hold old grudges.'

She was aware of Keir's quick glance then and bit her lip, wondering if he was applying those words to their own situation. But he merely said, 'I don't think it's hatred they're remembering, necessarily. It's courage. Malta was awarded the George Cross for the way she suffered and held firm during the war, Libby. That's something nobody need forget. Something they deserve to be proud of.'

They crossed the road and walked into Valletta's main street. There was no traffic here, but the warm evening air was filled with the hubbub of voices as a crowd of shoppers and sightseers mingled on the pavements, thronging the shop doorways, gossiping in little groups, their voices loud and unintelligible as they chattered and laughed in the strange Maltese language, a mixture it seemed of every language that this island had been forced to learn during its long history of occupation by one race and another. Again, the shops were bright with sparkling lights, each one an Aladdin's cave; Libby saw glass and china of a quality she had only previously seen in Bond Street stores, and the jewellery and perfumes made her gasp.

The street seemed to have been built along the spine of a ridge that ran eventually down to the sea, enclosing the famous Valletta harbour, and as they passed narrow streets on either side Libby could see the water below. The streets were more accurately described as stairways, she thought, with wide, shallow steps taking them down the steep sides of the ridge, and people were moving about below, evidently along other, lesser thoroughfares.

But she wasn't really taking all this in. She was too acutely aware of the man at her side, the man who walked close but without touching her except when their arms, loosely swinging, brushed and that tingle, so exciting and so dangerous, prickled its way through Libby's body. And she was too aware of all those questions that had not yet been answered. Or even asked.

Keir took her to a small, dimly-lit restaurant in a side street. Their table was by the window, overlooking the harbour with the lights of the city now reflected in the dark, hammered pewter of the water. Tiny points of brightness that must be boats, moving gently on the slow swell; occasionally, one could be seen wending its way through the moored vessels, off on a fishing trip perhaps.

It was fish that they ate as their main course. On Keir's advice, Libby chose melon to start with—they were particularly delicious here, he told her, and some of the other starters, like cannelloni or spaghetti, would probably prove substantial enough to count as a main course. Looking at one or two of the other tables, Libby decided he was probably right. She wanted to try the seafood Malta was famous for anyway, and feeling very daring she plumped for swordfish.

It came with chips and salad—another of Britain's legacies, she thought wryly—but she enjoyed the firm, creamy texture of the fish, and enjoyed too the wine that Keir had chosen to go with it. Something local, she could never remember quite what it was called, but it was pleasant and eased her tension so much that she was able at last to smile naturally across the table at Keir and respond when he began to talk about their engagement again.

'Remember the time we went to Hay Tor and climbed the rock?' he was asking, his blue eyes smiling at the memory. 'You got stuck at the top and couldn't get down—or pretended you couldn't, I was never quite sure. And then we went to Becka Falls and I photographed you by the water. It was pretty there, and unspoilt, but we didn't like Dartmeet so much, remember? That huge car park and the wire fences . . .'

'It was better when we walked along the river,' she said, joining in at last. 'So many people just go there and stay by the car park and the clapper bridge, if you just walk a little way you can be quite alone.'

'I know,' he said, and his eyes rested on her face. 'I remember that, too.'

Libby felt her colour rise in her cheeks. She had forgotten how they had walked, arms wound round each other, beside the river Dart, leaving the crowds behind. But now the memory flooded back. She was there again, slipping down into the heathery hollow to lie close to Keir, hearing the river chuckle past as they kissed, letting their bodies mould together as lips met and spoke a language more subtle than words, and hands moved in tender exploration of contours that were already well-known.

That had been one of the times when only Keir's strength of mind had kept them from that final capitulation to the yearning that shook them both. Even when Libby's body had arched almost involuntarily towards him, begging him to complete their lovemaking, he had refused, telling her again that for her it had to be perfect, marred by nothing.

'It would be perfect now,' she whispered as the feathery clouds wheeled above them in the eggshell-blue sky. 'Here in the heather, with the sun warm on our skins—please, Keir, please . . .'

But he only smiled that tender smile that made her want him even more and kissed her gently before pulling away from her and buttoning her shirt with long, sensitive fingers.

'It will be even more perfect on our wedding-night,' he promised. 'I'll make sure of that. And it's not so very far away—only two more weeks now. We can wait, my darling.'

And they had waited—for a wedding-night that never came. Tears filled Libby's eyes suddenly and she looked down quickly, praying that none would fall. Why had she had to remind Keir of that afternoon in particular? Or had he reminded her? She was too confused to know, now. She only knew that they had to stop all this reminiscing and talk—talk about why she was here, and what was going to happen next.

Keir's hand came across the table and gripped hers, and she was startled by the urgency of his clasp. Involuntarily, she looked up and met his dark blue gaze.

'We were happy, weren't we, Libby?' he asked, and she nodded, incapable of denying it, knowing that it would be a kind of betrayal to do so. Her heart jumped suddenly—was he really trying to tell her he wanted a reconciliation, that he loved her still? But she remembered his odd mood of the afternoon and cautioned herself to be wary. Even this could be part of his revenge, if she had been right in suspecting that. Don't jump too quickly, she thought. Let him come out into the open first

Keir's eyes were still on her, dark and intent, and she waited with a thumping heart for what he would say next. This was the moment, she was sure of it. She was conscious of his hand over hers, his fingers warm and strong on her wrist. He could probably feel the way her blood was racing, feel the pounding pulse beneath his fingertips. He had always known her almost too well—always been able to tell when her desire for him was rising.

Keir opened his mouth to speak, but another voice got in first, and there was a moment of absolute stillness as they both realised that the waiter was there, asking if everything was all right, smiling at them with a friendliness that at that moment neither of them reciprocated.

Damn him, Libby thought with a quite uncharacteristic viciousness. *Damn* him! And now it might be hours before we can reach that point again.

Keir gave her a small, rueful grin as he asked for the bill and paid, and then they walked out into the darkened street. There were fewer people about now; the steep little alley-ways leading down to the harbour had a sinister look to them and the Opera House was an eerie ruin under the moon. Neither of them spoke as they walked across to the car park; the drive back to Zurrieq was equally silent. Libby shivered and pulled her light jacket around her, feeling suddenly chilled.

They went up to the flat and Keir switched on the two big pottery floor lamps that lit the room with a gentle glow. The picture window was dark now, a panel of black in the silvery-green walls, but Keir didn't draw the long curtains that matched the cool colouring of the room. Instead, he walked over to a bar in one corner and asked Libby what she would like to drink.

'Oh—nothing strong,' Libby said in sudden alarm—she must keep a cool head, and she had already had quite a lot of wine. 'Keir—' she watched as he made the drinks and brought them across to the window '—Keir, we've got to talk.'

'I know.' His eyes held hers as he touched glasses, then he moved away very slightly and Libby sank into a chair. Her heart was jumping painfully. Keir watched her for a moment as if trying to make up his mind about something; then, the decision apparently made, he spoke abruptly.

'Libby. You asked me earlier why I'd asked you to come out here, to Malta. I wouldn't answer you then—' he paused again, weighing up his words while Libby waited breathlessly. '—and I'm afraid I'm not going to answer you now,' he went on devastatingly. 'Because I can't.'

'You—you *can't*?' Bewilderment shook her first, then anger. 'What do you mean, you can't? Did you bring me all this way to play some foul game with me, Keir? Because if you did, I can only say it's the lowest, filthiest trick I've ever heard of. What's got into you? What's *twisted* you? What happened between us was over two years ago, Keir—can't you forget it?' She ignored the spasm almost of agony that creased his face and went on remorselessly. 'Sally was right, I should never have come. I should have ignored that letter—torn it up and thrown it away and pretended it had never arrived.'

She paused, panting for breath. All the bewilderment of the past few days, the unanswered questions, the pain of old memories re-awakened, came together in a tight knot of anguish. The only release was to attack; but words had run out on her and all she could do was glare at him, hating him with her eyes and the rigid tension of her body.

Keir stared at her and she wanted to slap him. Was he now going to pretend he didn't understand? What the hell was all this about?

'Letter?' Keir repeated, and she sighed with exasperation. 'What letter?'

'Oh, for goodness' sake! The letter you wrote me, of course! The letter asking—*begging*—me to come out here. Or maybe you don't remember,' she added cuttingly. 'Maybe it's just slipped your memory that you wrote me a letter. Convenient—but not very likely to convince, Keir. Because I just happen to have brought it with me. So you can't get out of it that way.'

To her surprise, he didn't try. He just turned away, passing a hand across his forehead as if sick of the whole thing. And that makes two of us, she thought viciously, watching him as she wondered what his next trick would be. Well, whatever it was, she knew one thing for certain. Tomorrow morning, first thing, she would be at the airport for the first available flight home. She wasn't going to stay here to be made a fool of for a moment longer than she had to.

'Look,' Keir said, speaking as if trying to make sense of the tangle himself—only that was crazy, since he'd set the whole thing up. 'You may not believe this, but the first thing I knew about you coming here was *your* letter. The one you wrote to me. It arrived yesterday and all you said was that you were coming and the time of your flight in. I had no idea why you were coming—no idea about anything. Except,' he added, almost too softly for her to hear, 'that I was damned glad about it.'

Libby ignored that. She gave a snort of disbelief. 'Didn't know I was coming? Oh, try something better than that, Keir! You *wrote* to me—I've got the letter! You can't deny it. I'd know your handwriting anywhere. What's the *point*?' She jumped to her feet and ran into the bedroom, scrabbling through a drawer and returning with the sheet of paper clutched in her hand. 'Look. *Look!* Can you really stand there and tell me that's not your writing? Can you really deny that you wrote it? *Can you?*'

She pushed the sheet at Keir and stood back, trembling, while he stared at it. She couldn't help biting her lip at its crumpled state—would he guess that it was because of the times she'd read it? But it was unmistakably his, the writing firm and black across the page. He couldn't say it wasn't—could he?

At last Keir looked up. Their eyes met and she saw that pain in his again, the pain she had noticed and wondered about earlier. What *had* happened to him, to make him look like that—as if he were haunted? And was it anything to do with this letter, and his strange behaviour since her arrival?

'Well?' she challenged him, unable to stand the tension any longer.

Keir shook her head slowly. He held out the sheet of paper and looked at it again.

'*Well?*' she bit out. 'Are you still going to deny it? Are you *still* going to say that you didn't write that letter?'

He shrugged, almost helplessly. Then he sighed, as if he had no alternative and said simply: 'All I can say, Libby, is that *to my knowledge* I didn't write this letter. I'm sorry, but that's the fact. I have no recollection at all of writing these words.'

'You—you *what*?' Libby struggled for words. 'You *have no recollection*? *To your knowledge*—what kind of an answer is that? Can't you even give a straight reply? Can't you say yes or no, or are you still trying to twist things, still trying to make black look white?'

He shook his head again. 'I'm not trying to twist anything, Libby. I'm not in any position to. What I've just told you is thc truth—I don't have any recollection of writing this letter. Because I don't have any recollection of anything that's happened in the past two years. It's all a blank, Libby. One long, grey blank.'

CHAPTER THREE

LIBBY'S grey eyes clouded with bewilderment as she stared at Keir. Her slender fingers trembled slightly as she ran them through the feathers of dark hair that framed her puzzled face, and she shook her head slightly, wondering if she could possibly have heard aright.

'A blank?' she repeated. 'Are—are you saying that you don't remember? You don't remember writing me that letter?'

'That's exactly what I'm telling you,' he said, and his deep voice was ragged. 'I don't remember a thing about it—although I quite obviously *did* write it, I'm not trying to deny it. And it's not only that I've forgotten—as I told you, as far as I'm concerned the past two years just haven't happened. They're a complete blank. It's as if the entire world is playing some giant confidence trick on me in telling me they've passed at all.'

Libby sank back into her chair. She felt totally lost. Could this really be true—or was Keir himself playing a confidence trick on *her*? And for what reason? But no, surely that couldn't be the case. He wasn't that kind of man—was he?

'You'll have to tell me all about it,' she said at last. 'What caused it—just what *can* you remember? And why do you think you sent for me, if you can't remember doing it?' She looked at him again, eyes wide and smoky in her white face. 'Can I be of any help, or am I just going to make things worse by staying?'

Keir shrugged, and she could have sworn that he was as bewildered as she was herself. The skin was stretched finely against his cheekbones and over his temples, and she realised with a pang that his haunted look could be caused only by the forgotten ghosts of his own past.

'I'll tell you what I know, Libby,' he said slowly. 'It's the least I can do. And maybe you can tell me a few things that will help—though whether you stay or not will have to be your decision. You see—I don't know what broke us up. I don't know what's been happening to you since my last memory, two years ago.' He paused, and then added with a quietness that drove a shaft of fear into Libby's heart: 'I don't know what's happened to me.'

'You—you mean there might have been other women?' Libby whispered, and he gave her a sardonic glance.

'What do *you* think? I'm pretty sure there *have* been other women—I've never been the kind of man to live like a monk, I know *that*. But—' he shrugged again, looking suddenly helpless '—the way I feel now, the way I felt two years ago, there's only been one woman who really mattered.' His eyes, dark as sapphires, rested on her face with a bald hunger. 'You.'

A tiny gasp escaped from between Libby's parted lips. Keir was telling her he loved her, loved her as much as he'd loved her before the break-up of their engagement two years ago. Her heart leapt—and then chilled as she realised the warning behind his words. What *had* happened during the past two years? Had he fallen in love with someone else—and if so, when he regained his memory, would he still be in love with her? Or would his rediscovered love for Libby endure?

'How—how did it happen?' she asked, moistening dry lips. 'Did you have some kind of accident?' She had only a hazy idea as to how people lost their memories, but wasn't it usually the result of a knock on the head?

Keir nodded ruefully. 'A water-skiing accident, or so they tell me—I don't even remember that. I can believe it, though, from the bruises I had afterwards. Broke a couple of ribs, too, but they've mended now. All I've got are some blurred recollections of being in hospital, gradually clearing—and then the realisation that I didn't seem to have any life before that. Everything was a blank at that stage—I knew nothing at all, even my own name. It was almost like being born—I didn't even know there was any reason why I *should* remember anything. I could have been starting life—it might even have been the normal start to any life, for all I knew.'

He paused and Libby watched him silently, her mind filled with the horror of it. It had never occurred to her that a lost memory might be quite so obliterating. In all the stories she had read, the person had known all about everyday life—she had never heard of anyone's memory being so completely and horrifyingly wiped out as this.

'Fortunately that stage didn't last long,' Keir went on. 'I suppose anyone who's been knocked out for any length of time experiences it to some degree—even the confusion as you recover from an anaesthetic must be much the same. I just had it a bit worse and a bit longer. But after two or three days I knew enough to realise just what I *didn't* know.'

'But it did come back?' Libby whispered. 'At least—you know who you are, everything about yourself.'

'Everything except the last two years,' he reminded her. 'And I've got a feeling they're important . . . It didn't come back all at once. It came back in patches—a bit here, a bit there. And at the same time I was losing new bits—bits that happened *after* the accident. I'd do something one day and have no recollection of it the next. I guess that's what happened about your letter. Obviously, I wrote it—and I know I meant every word.

But I forgot it almost immediately. And until your letter came, saying that you were on your way, I'd no idea I would ever see you again.' His voice dropped as he said: 'It was like a bolt from the blue. I couldn't believe it. I didn't know what to make of it.'

There was a tiny silence; then Libby asked in a low voice: 'Just what do you remember, Keir? About us?' And found her heart thumping unevenly as she waited for his answer.

Keir's eyes burned into hers as he looked at her. For a moment, a long, endless moment, she wanted to throw herself into his arms, tell him that it didn't matter, none of it mattered, she was here now and they were together and could forget that past—remember only what they wanted to remember, both of them—but a new caution held her back. Once, she would have done just that. But two years had gone by since then; she was older and wiser, perhaps a little cynical. This was a situation she had never dreamed of; she must hold back, must tread very, very warily. She couldn't risk getting hurt again.

'What do I remember?' Keir said musingly. 'Oh, I remember so much—every detail of those few months, as sharply as if they'd just happened. As far as I'm concerned, they *have* only just happened, you see! But my last memory is of that day on the moors—the one we were talking about earlier.' He stopped, then added: 'I remember lying in the heather with you and wanting you so badly—and then there's nothing until I found myself here on Malta, in the hospital, and you no longer anywhere in my life.'

The silence was longer this time as Libby tried to assimilate all that he had told her. If it were true, she knew more of Keir's life since their break-up than he did himself. Admittedly, she knew only what she had read in gossip columns, but Keir didn't even seem to know that.

Could he really be totally unaware of all that had happened? The quarrel—the pain—the aftermath?

And the way he had spent his life since then? The books he had written—the women he had known?

And one woman in particular—the Italian countess, Pia. Could he really have forgotten her?

Feeling her way as delicately as a cat treading on unfamiliar ground, she said: 'Haven't you any idea at all? I mean, there must be people on Malta who know you, who can tell you why you're here, things like that. Doesn't that help?'

'Up to a point, it does.' Keir stood up and moved restlessly across the room to stand silhouetted against the wide window. 'I know I'm here to write a book on Malta and its history. I've got my notes and I can pick up and go on with that, although I have to go over a lot of the ground again—my notes are too sketchy in some places, where I was obviously relying on my own memory.' His mouth twisted at the phrase. 'I've got a good friend here too, who's been able to tell me quite a lot about what's happened in the blank time.' Libby felt her heart twist at those words. Surely he could only mean a woman—the exotic Pia, perhaps—and if so, her own position was going to be impossible.

But Keir went on without noticing her sudden flush. 'But being *told* isn't the same as actually *remembering*. I can accept it, believe it even—but I don't *know* it. It's not personal experience any more.' He paused and she saw the frown of concentration as he tried to find words to explain. 'It's like hearing about someone else. My own emotions aren't involved—in a way, I suppose I've lost them too, and that's the worst thing of all. Losing your emotions.'

And when you regain them, Libby thought. When the memory comes back—as surely it must—and those emotions with it. How would Keir feel about her then—when he recalled the quarrel that had broken them apart?

Perhaps it would be better for all concerned if she left now—got out of his life, and got him out of hers, before the worst happened.

'That's why it's so incredible that you're here,' Keir said softly, coming to stand before her, his eyes the deep blue of the night sky outside. 'And it's why those two years suddenly don't seem so important. Because whatever's happened, it's brought us together again—given us the chance to start again.' A sudden anxiety creased his forehead and he dropped down beside her, his hands urgent on her arms as the dark eyes bored into hers. 'We *can* start again, can't we, Libby? There's no one else? You—' his hand slid down to her own and turned it palm downwards '—you're not married, or engaged or anything? You're still free?'

'Free?' Libby struggled to retain control. His fingers were like fire on her bare arms, his breath was warm and sweet on her cheek, and his lips were altogether too close. It couldn't happen—not this way, however much she wanted it. And she did want it, she had to admit that even in the midst of the turmoil in her mind. She wanted Keir now just as much and as badly as she'd wanted him on that summer afternoon by the chuckling river on Dartmoor . . . But it mustn't happen—not now. 'Keir, wait—you can't spring all this on me and expect everything to be the same between us. We broke up, remember—?' She bit her lip. 'I mean, you *know* we did—you must know, even if you don't actually remember. I—'

'I didn't know,' he reminded her. 'Not when I received that letter. To me, then, we were still engaged—still committed to each other.'

'But you knew afterwards,' Libby said slowly, trying

to recall every word he had said since her arrival—was it only a few hours ago? 'You knew before I arrived that we'd broken up. So—'

'And what made you think that?' he broke in. Then he let go of her arm and brushed back his glinting gold hair with an impatient gesture. 'All right, I knew that something *had* gone wrong—or we'd have been married by now. And I knew that we weren't—don't ask me how, I just did know that. But what there was left—well, I had no idea, how could I have? And when I got your letter saying you were coming—remember, I didn't know I'd written to you—well, I thought everything must be okay. I thought we must have made it up, come together again. And then you arrived—and you looked at me like I was a ghost.' Libby, staring at him, remembering his words. *Don't look at me as if I'd come back from the dead.*

'I kissed you, and you held back from me. You didn't respond. Hell, Libby, can't you imagine what I was going through? Why did you come if we hadn't made up whatever we'd quarrelled about? I couldn't understand it. And you spoke to me as if I were a stranger—when you spoke at all. Was I on holiday, was this my flat? Polite little questions that nearly drove me to breaking-point.' He stood up, breathing hard, and Libby's hands crept to the arms of her chair and held them tightly. She could understand only too well how he must have felt. He must have been as bewildered as she.

'That's why I tried to talk about our engagement—I had to find out. But you stonewalled me at every point. You just wouldn't co-operate. Until that very last moment—and then we had to be interrupted by that damned waiter.' His mouth twisted in a mirthless grin. 'I thought we were beginning to find our way back then. Were we, Libby?'

He was beside her again, and Libby felt panic stab at her breast. He mustn't touch her—it was going too fast, she needed to think. With a quick movement, she got up from the chair, slipping past Keir to the window and staring out into the darkness. A tiny pinpoint of light showed somewhere out at sea and then disappeared. She was acutely conscious of the steady thump of her heart, the roar of blood in her ears.

'Keir, you're not giving me a chance,' she said unsteadily. 'It's all been a shock—I can't take it all in that quickly. And I need to know more. You say you've a friend here who's been able to help you—' she wanted to ask *what friend* but couldn't '—can't he—*she*—tell you these things? I haven't seen you for two years, Keir—how can I help? I know nothing—practically nothing—about what you've been doing. I . . .'

'I'm not asking you to help me,' he said quietly, and she could see his reflection in the dark glass, tall and slender, watching her with a look that was disturbingly intent. 'I'm just telling you how it's been. And telling you how it is for me—and you.'

'And your friend?' Libby asked, knowing that she had to face whatever truth there might be.

'My friend is a man,' Keir told her. 'His name's Jeremy Brooke and he's been working with me—doing research, acting as secretary and that kind of thing.' His glance was bitter. 'I gave up having women secretaries some time ago—too much hassle. And they weren't too keen on the research sometimes.'

Thinking of some of his books, which had been set in remote and uncomfortable corners of the earth, Libby could see his point. So Jeremy Brooke was the one who knew about Keir's life in the past two years. But what about Pia?

'Jeremy's told me some of what I need to know,' Keir

went on in a flat tone. 'But the rest of it—well, I haven't wanted to be told. I need to remember it by myself—not persuade myself I can remember, because I want to. If he tells me, that might happen and I can't risk it.' His eyes burned into her mind. 'I can't risk anything that might drive us apart again, Libby.'

Libby found her voice. 'Apart? But we aren't together!' She raised both palms to her face and found her cheeks hot. 'We broke up, Keir, can't you understand that? The fact that you've forgotten it doesn't make it any less real. We quarrelled—bitterly—it was all over. How do you know you won't feel the same when you *do* remember? How do you know that you don't really hate me?'

Keir was at her side almost before the words were out of her mouth, his arms gripping her close to him. The breath gasped out of her body as she stared up at him, and then his mouth was crushing down on hers, suppressing her exclamation, allowing no resistance. And as delight and horror blended in her veins, Libby clung to him, unable to pull away, conscious only of his arms holding her close, his body lean and hard against her own soft curves.

She felt his lips move with purpose over hers, parting them with an expertise that shot a pang of sweet memory through her. His hands slid over her body, one tightening over her breast, the other curving to the shape of her bottom, drawing her close in against him so that she could be in no doubt as to his desire, and her own flared to match it.

A tiny moan escaped her lips as his own freed them to nibble their way gently across her cheek to her earlobe, and she turned her head blindly, seeking his mouth again, lost to all reason, lost to everything but the sensations that had been missing from her life for two long years and were now surging within her like a tidal wave which there could be no stopping.

'Now do you believe I don't hate you?' Keir murmured as his tongue flicked in her ear. 'Do you really think I *could* hate you—even if I'd forgotten it—and hold you like this?'

Libby stayed quite still. Then she tilted her head back and looked up into his sapphire eyes. They were serious, sincere—but she couldn't trust them. At this moment, she believed that Keir loved her as much as he had ever done. But when he remembered . . . what then? Would he still love her, when the truth was once again a part of his experience, when his emotions were once more returned to him?

Libby took a long time to fall asleep that night, and the sun was high when she awoke, though her room was still darkened by the shutters that were essential to keep out the fierce heat of the summer. For a few minutes she lay gazing sleepily around the dim, cool room, wondering where she was; and then she remembered and sat up with a jerk.

That was what it must have been like for Keir—that waking to bewilderment. Only for him it had lasted longer and been more confusing, and for him memory hadn't returned, either so quickly or so completely. For him, there were still gaps.

Libby got out of bed and padded over to open the shutters. Her room faced the sea, down the same valley that she had seen from the big window of the living-room; only the bathroom and kitchen faced the street. There was a balcony outside and she stepped on to it, feeling the sun warm on her skin.

The balcony ran along the length of the apartment, and she could see that the wide window of the living-room was open, but there was no sign of Keir. Relieved—Libby still needed time to think—she went back into her room to shower and dress. Thank goodness her room had its own shower and washbasin and she didn't have to use the bathroom; at least she wouldn't run the risk of meeting Keir before she was fully in command of herself.

Not that she'd been that last night, she thought ruefully, remembering the way he had held and kissed her and her burning response. She had almost given in then—told Keir that it didn't matter, that she was still in love with him and she was willing to go back two years and start again whatever had happened in the meantime.

But she hadn't; not quite. And after the night's sleep that he had at last allowed her, she knew that she had been right.

She *was* still in love with Keir Salinger—there was no doubt at all about that. But she couldn't go back and start again as if nothing had happened. Because things had happened—a lot of things. And two things in particular.

When Keir did, eventually, remember why they had quarrelled, he might well want her out of his life, as he'd walked out of hers. And it would be worse still when he remembered the other complication.

Pia. What had happened between her and Keir? Where was she now? Would she come back—and if she did, just what would Keir's reaction be?

Until these questions were answered there could be no future for Libby with Keir—if, indeed, there could ever be. And until he could accept this she had to tread very carefully. For his sake as well as for her own.

Libby sighed as she stepped into the shower and turned it on. This was a whole lot more complicated than she'd envisaged. And it might turn out, even now, that she had been as crazy as Sally had said she was, to come. But she knew too that she had had no real choice. She'd had to respond to that letter—even if Keir had had no idea he'd written it.

There was still no sign of Keir when Libby, wearing a fresh skirt and camisole top of vivid coral pink, went back out to the balcony and along to the living-room. There was a round white table on the balcony, with two chairs, but Keir had evidently eaten his breakfast and gone out. Not sure whether to feel deflated or relieved, Libby went through to the kitchen and found fruit juice, fresh bread and coffee. She carried it out to the sunshine and sat there, gazing abstractedly down the valley to the sparkling sea and thinking hard.

It hadn't been easy to persuade Keir to let her go last night. It hadn't even been easy to persuade herself—there was nothing she longed for more than to stay in his arms, feeling the close warmth of his body, letting his lips play havoc with her emotions, letting her own body respond to his as it had longed to do on that afternoon on Dartmoor. And this time, she guessed, Keir wouldn't have refused her—they could have gone on, glorying in each other, until their lovemaking reached that triumphant conclusion they both needed so desperately. And then—well, she supposed they'd have taken it from there, living just for the moment, reckless of the consequences.

She was almost sorry that they hadn't. It would have been something to keep, to remember; if, when Keir regained his memory, the worst happened and she found herself alone again, she would always have that moment of fulfilment, the knowledge that they had, even if for a short time, belonged to each other. Wouldn't it have been worth it?

There was no way of knowing. But Libby had suffered

enough anguish when she had lost Keir for the first time. She couldn't risk it again—knowing that it would be so much worse once she had truly known his love.

'You'll have to let me go, Keir,' she had told him quietly as he bent to kiss her again. 'We can't just dismiss what's happened. We've got to go slowly—carefully.' Her grey eyes searched his. 'Wouldn't it be better if we discussed it—if I told you what broke us up, what happened to us?'

But Keir had shaken his head. 'I don't want to know. I have to remember things for myself. Don't you see, Libby, I'd only hear *your* side—I still wouldn't know just how *I'd* felt, just what thoughts went through *my* mind at that time.' He watched her face. 'Could it have been so bad, Libby? You don't seem to bear any grudge.'

But she shook her head. There was no way of explaining just half of what had happened—it had to be all or nothing. It *had* been bad at the time, but—oh, it was all too difficult.

She played absently with her bread as her mind went back to those final days. It had all seemed so right at first, so easy. Keir, writing his book about the war, telling her that he wanted to interview some of the people who had actually survived concentration camps, find out what their experiences had been and how they felt about them now, forty years later. She, excited by the project and never thinking about the results of her action, telling him that her own father had been in such a camp, certain that although the doctor never normally spoke about his experiences he would be happy to do so to Keir.

'He thinks a lot of you, I know,' she said, 'and I'm sure he'd be able to tell you a lot. He'd just qualified as a doctor then, and he practised as one in the camp. That's all I know, really—he never talks about it. But for your book I'm sure he would.'

'Well, don't let's rush at it,' Keir said thoughtfully. 'Some of the survivors just want to blot out that time, forget it completely. I wouldn't want to distress him or make him feel pressurised.'

'Oh no, that'll be all right,' Libby said confidently. 'I'll ask him, if you like. I'm sure he won't refuse.'

'And that's just what I mean,' Keir said with an affectionate grin. 'The nicest kind of pressure—and the hardest to refuse. No, I'll ask him—and I'll ask him in such a way that he *can* refuse if he wants to. I might not be so kind to all my victims—but I can't have my future father-in-law alienated!'

He had made his request later that evening, when he and Dr Marsh were walking round the garden after supper. Libby hadn't worried about it at all, confident that her father would agree, and she had been pleased but not surprised when Keir told her as they said good-night that he was going to spend the next day with the doctor, making notes and even a tape-recording of the older man's reminiscences.

'I knew he'd agree,' she smiled, lifting her face for Keir's kiss. 'Who's a clever girl, then?'

But Keir had remained grave. 'I'm still not entirely sure it's a good idea. Your father's obviously got some harrowing memories and I don't know that it's a good idea to disturb them. He asked me not to mention this to your mother, Libby.'

'Oh well, that's all right,' she said carelessly. 'Mummy does fuss rather a lot. And she's got a bit of a thing about the war—doesn't like people talking about it. Perhaps she had some unpleasant experiences, too.'

'I don't know.' Keir was thoughtful. 'Well, he's a grown man and can make his own decisions, but somehow I rather wish you'd never told me about this. I've got a nasty feeling . . .' And then he had shrugged and laughed at himself and kissed her, and they had been happy.

The next day he had spent with her father, and when the two men emerged for supper Libby had been surprised and concerned to see how drawn and weary the older man had looked. Her mother had been concerned too; she had exclaimed and fussed, and insisted on an early night, and then she had come back to the living-room where Libby and Keir were listening to records, and demanded to know just what had been going on.

'William won't tell me a thing,' she complained, 'but it's obviously to do with you, Keir. Just what have you been doing in that study all day? You've worn him out and quite possibly made him ill, and I have a right to know.'

'Oh, Mummy, don't fuss—' Libby began, but Keir got up at once, looking anxious.

'I certainly hope he isn't ill, Mrs Marsh. I admit he seemed very tired. We've been talking all day and it can be very tiring. I really am sorry.'

'Talking? What about?' Mrs Marsh's face narrowed with suspicion. 'Just what is the sudden interest in my husband, Keir? Just what is it you've been talking about all day? Tell me!'

Keir glanced at Libby and shrugged. 'I did promise your husband that I wouldn't say—' he began reluctantly, and Mrs Marsh snorted. Libby, watching her, was struck with sudden fear. She had never seen her mother look like this—never seen quite that quality of anger in the thin, worn face.

'Mummy—' she began, but Mrs Marsh ignored her and addressed Keir, her voice sharp.

'It's the war, isn't it? You've been talking about the war—about that horrible camp and what went on there. Oh, God!' She covered her face with her hands. 'Can he never have any peace? Can he never forget? Why does it have to be dragged up, all over again?'

Libby scrambled up, but when she touched her mother the older woman turned on her as if she were a stranger. 'Don't touch me! Don't you realise the damage you may have done?' Her eyes burned in her face as she glared at them. 'All these years I've looked after my husband, knowing that he could never tell me adequately what he'd been through, knowing that he had to bear it alone. And I knew, too, that it was better buried. If he were forced to tell—it could destroy him.'

'*Destroy* him?' Libby whispered. 'But why? What's it all about?'

Her mother looked at her with something very like contempt. 'You wouldn't understand, Libby. You're too young—you didn't live through those times. But I did. I waited at home, knowing that he might never come back, knowing that he was going through hell and unable to do a thing to help. And when he did come back, I knew that his experiences had changed him for ever. He was never quite the same again and never would be. It was the same with a lot of others. Some never recovered; some went on, as your father did, to lead useful lives. But none of them were ever the same.'

'But why should it do such harm to talk about it?' Libby asked, and her mother turned away with a curiously defeated attitude.

'Because your father's memories, from what little he has told me, are peculiarly horrific—he was a doctor then, don't forget—and because talking about them, even thinking about them, has always been very distressing for him. And—' she turned back and Libby was shocked to see the despair in her face '—because he has a heart condition. He's been warned to take very great care. He mustn't *be* distressed.' She was almost out of the door before she turned again and spoke directly to Keir. 'I'm going up to him now. I don't want to have to come down again—will you lock up and see that everything's ready for the night?' She didn't wait for his answer but left the room, closing the door behind her, and in the silence they heard her footsteps going slowly and wearily up the stairs.

Dr Marsh had his first heart attack later that night, and two more the next day in hospital. He didn't recover from the third one and he died before Libby, telephoning frantically to Claire, could get back to his bedside. She found herself looking down at his body with a numb grief and a lasting sadness that she hadn't been there to say goodbye.

If Libby could have lost her own memory regarding the period following her father's death, she would gladly have done so. It wasn't just the grief and the misery of arranging the funeral, letting people know and making a hundred and one other arrangements—they were the normal events following any death. What made it all the worse was her mother's reaction, and the way it affected Libby and her relationship with Keir.

Rationally, she knew that Keir had been unaware of her father's condition, and she knew too that Dr Marsh had taken his own decision to talk about the past, knowing quite well what it might mean to him. There was no way that Keir could be blamed—but Mrs Marsh did blame him, and her bitterness had an inevitable influence on Libby just when she was at her most vulnerable.

'Why did you have to do it?' she cried one afternoon as they sat in the garden. 'Dragging it all up—what good can it do? Things like that are best forgotten, it can't help anyone to bring it all out again after so long.'

'Can't it? That's a matter of opinion,' Keir said

thoughtfully. He picked a stem of grass and began to chew it. 'It's forty years—more—since that last war began. Couldn't that have something to do with the fact that people *haven't* forgotten it—that they keep reminding each other with books and films and plays showing its horror and futility? These things happened, Libby, and we can't pretend they didn't. They're part of our past whether we like it or not, and I believe that we ought to keep the memory alive—not so that we can keep hatred alive, but so that it's less likely to happen again.'

'But did you have to drag Dad into it?' Libby asked bitterly. 'You must have realised there was some reason why he didn't want my mother to know. Couldn't you have let it go?' She turned her head and looked at the strong profile, the firm jaw and well-shaped mouth. 'No, I suppose you couldn't,' she said slowly, feeling a coldness creep over her body. 'You had a good story there and you knew it, and that was all that was important to you, wasn't it? Never mind that my father was getting old and tired, never mind that he was ill. Never mind that for forty years he'd tried to forget the horrors he'd seen. The story was all that mattered—the story that you could write down and sell and make money out of.' Anger shook her as she stood up and looked down at him. 'My mother's right—you insinuated yourself into our family for what you could get from us. Well, you've got it—and I hope you're satisfied!'

She turned away, but Keir was on his feet and gripping her arm before she could escape. His face was hard and angry now, and she felt a bolt of fear jerk through her heart as she looked up at him. She had never seen that expression before and she knew suddenly that Keir would be a bad man to cross. But she held her ground and stared up into the dark blue eyes, defiance in her own.

'You'll take those things back, Libby,' Keir grated, his fingers burning a ring of fire round her wrist. 'You know damned well they're not true—I didn't even know about your father until you told me yourself. I had no idea he was ill, or even that he was any more tired than any other country GP. If anyone should have seen that, don't you think it should have been you? You've known him all your life, after all. Or maybe you've already realised that—and you're taking it out on me because you can't take your own guilt.'

Libby drew in a sharp breath. She heard the crack of her palm across Keir's cheek almost before she realised what she was doing—and then she stepped back sharply, staring appalled at the livid marks across the tanned face.

Slowly, Keir raised his hand to his cheek, looking at his fingers almost as if he expected to see blood on them. His eyes narrowed as he looked at Libby, and she stepped further away, trembling from head to foot, wanting only to get away but somehow unable to turn and run.

'We'll pretend you didn't do that, Libby,' Keir said quietly. 'You've been through a lot in these past few days—we all have—and nobody's quite themselves. But I think in view of what you've said I'd better go back to London. I'm obviously no longer welcome here, and I don't particularly want to act as a painful reminder.' He turned away, then turned abruptly back. 'I won't get in touch, Libby—I'll leave that to you. You know where to find me—if you do decide you need me.'

He was gone before she could speak, and it was only twenty minutes before his car roared away down the drive. He had spoken to nobody before leaving—Mrs Marsh had been in her bedroom, where she had spent much of her time since the funeral—and he had left simply a note of sympathy and regret. There was nothing for Libby herself.

'Well, I can't say I'm sorry,' Mrs Marsh declared when Libby told her what had happened. 'I'm very disappointed in that young man. He's proved himself highly insensitive, as well as totally domineering, and that's a combination you're well out of, my dear. Put it down to experience and be thankful you found him out before it was too late. A broken engagement's better than an unhappy marriage.'

'Yes, of course,' Libby agreed; but a cold shadow lay over her heart and she wondered if it would ever lift into warmth again.

Libby had stayed in Devon until Claire's twins were a few weeks old. They had been born a fortnight after Dr Marsh's death, and Claire had taken some time to recover. But at last she declared herself fit again and Libby, realising that her mother too was quite able to take care of herself in spite of her continuing dependence on her daughter, agreed that the time had come for her to leave.

'Though I do seem to be leaving you with all the problems,' she confessed to Claire as they sat nursing a twin each. But her sister shook her head firmly.

'It's been a ghastly time for us all, but we've got to start living again, Mum included. And these two little scraps are helping a lot. She can't come over here expecting tea and sympathy—I just don't have time. Anyone who comes through my front door has to buckle to and help these days, and that does Mum the world of good. You get off back to your own life, Libby. You may feel you're abandoning her, but I'll bet that within less than a fortnight she'll be back to her old self and organising the whole village again. And we'll always let you know if you are needed.' She paused and glanced sideways at Libby. 'Anyway, it's your life that needs tidying up now. What about Keir? Have you heard from him?'

'No, and don't expect to.' Libby felt the cold settle round her heart as it always did when she thought of Keir. She hadn't really believed that he would simply walk out of her life—but he had. There had been no word since the day he had walked out of the garden and left her. 'It's all over, Claire. I think maybe Mum was right—he did make up to me just to get an introduction to Dad. Once he'd got his story—well, he couldn't get away fast enough.'

'Rubbish!' Claire said forcefully. 'I'll never believe that. All right, Lib, you're hurt now, but you must know in your heart that it's not true. Keir's just not that kind of man.'

Wasn't he? Libby shook her head despairingly, knowing that she had already asked herself that question a thousand times. She could have sworn that Keir's passion was genuine; that he'd sincerely loved her when he refused to take advantage of her own desire that day in the heather. But if he had loved her, would he have left her so abruptly, not given her a chance to make things up? She didn't know—she just didn't know.

And for the next two years, as time cleared the distortions of grief and Libby grew to realise that Keir really could not be blamed for her father's death, she still could find no answer to her question. Had he really loved her—and had she killed that love by turning on him in the way she had?

And if she had killed it, could it ever be revived? or had it gone for ever?

CHAPTER FOUR

It was after eleven when Keir returned, and Libby was still on the balcony, watching the distant sea and lost in her thoughts. The situation in which she found herself now was something she wasn't at all sure she could cope with, and she was wondering if she was wise to stay at all. Wouldn't it be better for her to return to London as soon as possible? Nothing had really changed between Keir and herself, after all—and neither of them had any idea as to how he had felt about her before his accident.

The thought of looking at Keir's face one day and realising that he had remembered everything, made her shiver. Suppose she saw hatred or contempt in his eyes? If that were his true feeling, she didn't want to know—she certainly didn't want to be here to see it.

As she heard Keir come through the entrance to the flat, she tensed, half afraid that he might already have remembered. Her eyes were wide as he came through the living-room, his easy stride reminding her of the loose-limbed but alert movements of a jungle beast, and she fluttered a glance at his face. But the shadow was still there in his eyes, like a shutter between him and the past, and Libby didn't know whether to be relieved or sorry.

'Oh, you're awake,' Keir remarked, dropping into the chair opposite her. He was more at ease today, more confident—and, somehow, more remote. Libby studied him surreptitiously, taking in the details of his immaculate cream slacks and blue shirt that echoed the sapphire tone of his eyes. The sun glinted on his hair, making it look like polished gold, and Libby felt a pang. It just wasn't possible that he hadn't been loved by more than one woman in two years—and wasn't it equally possible that he'd loved them, too? And the dark beauty of the Italian *contessa*, seen in a newspaper photograph, floated into her mind.

Keir poured himself some coffee and glanced across at her. His expression was quizzical, and slightly wary. He must be wondering just what she planned to do, Libby realised, and she plunged straight in to tell him.

'I'm going back to England, Keir. There isn't any point in my staying—it will only complicate things. Can you—do you know when the next flight is?'

Keir's eyes narrowed and she watched him, feeling the colour pulse into her cheeks. Perhaps she'd been too abrupt—but there was no point in beating about the bush. And Keir might even be relieved at her decision. He might have written to ask—beg—her to come, but he had been in a different state of mind then. He'd forgotten doing it, but he hadn't written again.

'Back to England?' he said. 'But why? You've come all this way—why turn round and go rushing back? What are you afraid of?'

Libby bit her lip. She couldn't answer that, couldn't tell him she was afraid of what might happen if she stayed, letting him believe he was still in love with her—and then seeing him remember the truth.

'I'm not afraid of anything,' she said insincerely. 'I just don't think there's any point—'

'But there's every point!' He reached out across the table, and Libby would have jerked her hand away if his fingers hand't been so gentle, so tenderly caressing. Hypnotised, she watched their slow movements over her own and tried to calm her racing pulse. 'Libby, this accident could prove to be the best thing that ever happened to us. Whatever's happened since, I've got back all the wonderful feeling of being in love with you. We can start again. Because you're in love with me too . . . aren't you, Libby? His thumb moved over her palm and Libby closed her eyes as an ache spread from her hand to her shoulder. 'You don't have to answer,' he went on, his voice like deep brown velvet caressing her mind as his fingers caressed her hand. 'I know you very well, Libby . . . there's not much you can hide from me. And why should you want to? We belong together, you and I. We nearly lost each other—why, I don't know—but now we're together again. We can't let this chance go by.' His fingers slid up her bare arm, setting up a tingle that spread an exquisite agony through to the very soles of her feet. 'Don't leave me now, Libby. Don't throw away our chance and spoil both our lives.'

Desperately, Libby clung to her senses, though they threatened to drown her in the whirlpool of primitive instinct. 'Keir, you can't say these things,' she protested, wishing that her voice didn't sound so half-hearted. 'You don't even know that they're true. You feel what you feel because you can't remember what's happened since. Suppose there's another girl—a girl with more right to your love than I have. You might be engaged—you might be *married*! Have you thought of that?' Her grey eyes misted as the thought occurred to her. Suppose Keir *was* married—then there would be no chance for her, no chance whatever.

But he was shaking his head positively. 'No, I'm not married, Libby. And if there has been anyone else—well, it was a mistake. It's what I feel for you that's real, and I'm not letting you go until you can see it too.'

'Not letting me go!' Libby half rose to her feet. 'Keir, you can't keep me here—not against my will—I—' But his fingers tightened round her wrist and she knew that if she struggled his strength would prove too much for her.

'Keir,' she said, trying to quieten her tone, 'you must see that this is an impossible position. I *can't* stay.'

'Can't? Why not? What is there to stop you?' He was on his feet too, close to her, the inevitable weakness assailing her as she felt his closeness. 'Libby, you can't run out on me now. I need you—'

'*Now*, perhaps,' she flashed. 'But what about later—when you remember? Suppose you find you don't need me after all? You can't be sure that won't happen—it could happen next week, it could happen tomorrow, even today—'

'Or it might never happen at all.' His eyes burned into hers, blue fire meeting grey smoke. 'Those two years might never come back, Libby. Are you going to destroy us because of something that might never happen—might never *have* happened?'

Libby turned her face away, feeling helpless. Keir had always been able to overpower her with words, and that was something that hadn't changed. For a moment she wondered if she should do as he wanted—forget the past two years as completely as he had forgotten them, go on from that sunny day by the river. But if she did, there would have to be explanations—she would have to tell him about her father and about the quarrel. And she couldn't face that—couldn't face telling Keir about the thing that had split them apart and watch him listening as if to a story about someone else.

'Please, Keir, let me go,' she said in a low voice, and she felt his grip on her wrist ease so that his fingers enclosed it only loosely.

'All right, Libby.' His voice was equally quiet. 'If that's what you really want. But be very sure. And if it's not—well, why not just stay and have a holiday? Start right from the beginning, if you like—get to know each other all over again.' His eyes crinkled suddenly. 'Look, you must admit you have a golden opportunity—if you do still have any feeling for me. Everything's on your side. You're here and I'm crazy about you. As far as I'm aware there isn't anyone else, and nobody else has come rushing to my side. So what have you got to lose?' His eyes darkened in a way that made Libby's heart jump. 'I think you'll regret it if you go home, Libby.'

Aware that she was struggling against a force greater than herself, Libby laughed uncertainly and said: 'You have a very good opinion of yourself, Keir, even if you have lost your memory.'

'No, as a matter of fact, I haven't,' he said thoughtfully. 'But I know you very well, Libby, and I know your responses. Your lips may not tell me you love me in words, but they can't hide the fact in other ways . . .' And before she could move, he drew her close and placed his mouth firmly over hers. Libby gave a tiny moan as the familiar fire licked through her body, melting all resistance, and she felt her arms go round him, her hands slide up his back to tangle in the thick gold hair. Keir muttered something deep in his throat as he gathered her closer against him, so that their bodies met and merged and, through the thin cotton of her dress, Libby could feel every outline of his hard body. A sharp pain of longing pierced her heart, and she clung to him, whimpering as his hands slid down her body to find the sweet curves that moved so responsively under his touch.

Then he drew away, still holding her close against him and tilting her chin with one finger so that she was forced to meet his eyes. Her soft lips trembled as she looked up at him through a haze of tears, and he nodded slightly, as if satisfied.

'You do still love me, Libby,' he murmured, 'and you'll stay on Malta with me . . . won't you? Oh, don't panic—' he held up his hand as Libby struggled to speak '—I'm not going to force you. I can understand your feelings, I can see why you're afraid. Look, I'll make a bargain with you.' He let her go then and moved away, a few inches that seemed like miles, leaning against the balustrade and watching her. 'Stay with me and we'll just take it easily, getting to know each other as I said, and I promise I won't try to rush things. Will that make you happier? You'll have all the time in the world to make up your mind—to see if you think it's real, to find out if you can trust me if you like to put it that way. And then we'll think again. How does that strike you?'

'I—I don't know.' Libby moved back to her chair and sank into it as if she had just run a marathon. 'I don't think I can cope if you—'

'If I kiss you like that again?' He made a rueful face. 'Well, I said I wouldn't rush things. I won't touch you again—not until you're ready. It won't be easy—I want to have you in my arms as a permanent fixture—but if it'll help . . .'

'And if you remember?' Libby asked softly.

Keir's eyes moved over her, almost assessingly. Then he said: 'If I remember, Libby, you'll be the first to know. I promise you that. But I'm as sure as I'm sure I'm standing here that it won't make one iota of difference. Not as far as you and I are concerned.'

I wish I could be sure, Libby thought. She looked down the valley, watching the gaily-coloured specks that Keir had told her were boats taking trippers to the Blue Grotto. People on holiday, people without a care in the world . . . Should she do as Keir had asked? Stay here with him, risking pain greater than any she had known before, but taking the chance also of regaining a happiness she had believed to be lost for ever? Was she being wise—or incredibly, crazily foolish?

But even as she wondered, she knew the answer. She'd known it all the time, or she wouldn't have flown out here, to Malta, against everyone's advice. She wouldn't have stayed last night, or be here now talking with Keir—letting him kiss her . . .

'All right,' she said, looking past him so that she shouldn't see the expression in his eyes. 'I'll stay—for a while at least.'

The sun was hot on Libby's shoulders as she settled herself beside Keir in the front seat of his car. Even now, she wasn't certain she had made the right decision, but Keir had shown his delight so plainly that she'd been unable to retract. And as he had also stood by his promise not to touch her again, she felt, with some relief, that she might just be able to cope with his nearness. And it was difficult to continue to worry with the sun shining and a delicious warmth pervading the air—especially when she remembered that back in England the leaves were changing colour and it was probably raining. Why not do as Keir had suggested—treat it as a holiday and see what happened?

'If I'm going to stay I might as well do something useful,' she had offered as they ate a simple lunch of bread, cheese, ham and olives. 'Can I help with your research? I know you've got your secretary—Jeremy, did you say his name was?—but if you've got to do it all over again you might be glad of some help.'

'Hm. Not a bad idea, so long as you can stand it.' Keir looked at her with appreciation. 'As I said, I've got some notes but they're a bit sketchy, so I'd intended going back over all the ground. If you wouldn't mind helping me with that, it would leave Jeremy free for what he was doing already—the more advanced stuff, looking at old documents, and so on. He's particularly good at that kind of thing, while I prefer getting my own impressions from what I can actually see. It includes trailing around a lot of ancient monuments, that kind of thing—think you could take it?'

'Oh yes, I'm very interested in that sort of thing. Remember the standing stones on Dartmoor?' Libby spoke without thinking of the memories they shared, then blushed as she caught Keir's eye on her. 'What kind of book is it, exactly?' she hurried on.

'Basically, it's a history of the island, but I want to bring out certain features. The way the Maltese have always remained themselves, whoever was ruling them; the courage that's lasted through the ages, culminating in their bravery during the last war. There's something in these people, Libby, some characteristic that belongs peculiarly to them and which seems to get diluted when they leave their own island. Perhaps when I've worked my way through their history and written it all down as it appears to me, I might reach some kind of answer. That's the challenge of it, of course.'

'Yes, I see. It sounds fascinating.' Libby was beginning to feel quite excited by the project. 'Where do we start?'

Keir grinned. 'Well, I already *have* started,' he pointed out. 'But I want to have a look at some of the ancient temples, and I'll need to see Mdina and the catacombs at Rabat. Amongst a lot of other things! Fortunately, nothing on Malta is very far from anywhere else and I don't really need to research chronologically—wherever we go, there's likely to be something of interest, so you can enjoy your holiday, too.'

He had decided to start by taking Libby to the temple of Hagar Qim. This was, he explained, just one of the many ancient temples on the island, and one of the most complex. 'Puts Stonehenge in the shade,' he remarked, and when they reached it Libby saw what he meant.

She got out of the car and looked with awe at the great megaliths, some of them over twenty feet high, still in the formation of the rooms and apses that had made up the original temple. Keir led her through the entrance and she stared around at the uneven blocks that formed the façade, the walled passages and the altar slabs. This must have been even more impressive when it was first built, and she tried to imagine the people of the time, labouring with no more than primitive tools to raise a temple to their god. It was open to the sky now, but she supposed that there had once been a roof, perhaps even a higher storey. How long had it taken to build, she wondered, and for how many centuries had men worshipped there?

'It dates back to 2400 to 2000 BC,' Keir told her as they roamed around the complex, peering through niches and into unexpected alcoves. 'Around four thousand years old, in fact. Not all that long when you think of man's time on earth. They'd had time to learn quite a lot. They weren't by any means primitive—their society must have been highly-structured to have envisaged and undertaken such a project as this.'

'And I suppose their society stayed the same for quite a long time,' Libby said thoughtfully. 'It's only in the past few hundred years that there have been really rapid changes—and in this century particularly.'

'That's right. Before that, you could probably have roamed about in time over quite a few thousand years and not seen very much difference.'

Libby paused and looked out, past the great stones, to the sea that danced and sparkled its way into the distance. The whole of Malta was a fortress, a rocky bastion standing alone in the ocean, rising sheer from the ocean floor to end abruptly in towering cliffs hundreds of feet high. The people who built this temple must have thought it impregnable; but it was its very impregnability that had made it such a coveted jewel. If you held Malta, you could command the Mediterranean, she had heard, and she could believe in the truth of that. No wonder it had been such a prized possession, and no wonder so many nations had tried to possess it.

Afterwards, Keir took her down a winding road that led breathtakingly to the foot of the cliffs to a tiny inlet, surrounded by towering rocks, with a small beach where people were still swimming even though the sun had almost gone. This, he told her, was Ghar-Lapsi and it was still used as a fishing-harbour, though there was nothing there but a restaurant and a car park.

'You'll see the fish brought in here during the day being sold in the markets in the evening,' Keir said. 'Or perhaps in the streets, early in the morning—there's a woman who walks through Zurrieq every day with a pram full of fish, calling out for people to come and buy. That's the time to shop, incidentally—at six in the morning. The women get up early to go to church and shop on the way home, before the heat of the day and while things are still fresh.'

'But it isn't too hot now,' Libby remarked. 'And it's been lovely this afternoon.'

'Ah, but this is October, almost November. You'd find it a good deal hotter in August. And it can get quite chilly in the middle of the winter, though Malta never gets the frost and snow that England suffers from.'

They walked along the cliff paths until dark, then turned back and went into the restaurant for a meal. It wasn't a restaurant of character, like the one in Valletta, but the food was good and the view across the moonlit sea was tranquilly beautiful. Libby could feel her stretched nerves relax; perhaps after all she had done right. She smiled across the table at Keir and wished she could take away that shadow that still lurked behind his eyes.

But it was too soon for that. Instead, she said: 'Tell me more about these ancient temples. How many are there?'

'Eight major ones, accessible to the public,' Keir answered. 'You've seen one of the best at Hagar Qim. They seem to be shrines to some kind of fertility cult—remember I told you about the figures that were found at Hagar Qim, the "fat lady" and other fertility symbols—they appear at the others, too. There's a very fat lady indeed in the temple at Tarxien, and some rather Disney-like piglets having their breakfast. But those aren't the only prehistoric sites. There's an underground temple, the Hal-Saflieni Hypogeum, in Paola, not far from Valletta; it's very similar to the other temples, but it's been carved out of rock rather than built—an even greater achievement, I'd say. I'll take you to see it.'

'I've heard of the catacombs, but I'd never heard of that,' Libby said. 'And Hagar Qim seemed much more complex than any of the temples I've seen in other countries.'

'Oh yes, they're all unique to Malta. They may even have influenced other European building—quite a lot of people believe that they date from rather earlier than I told you this afternoon. But they aren't the only curiosities, you know.' And he went on to tell her about other strange things to be found on the island—the dolmens, the rock tombs used over five thousand years ago and, most mysterious of all, the so-called cart ruts—long, parallel grooves in the bare rock believed to have been made by 'slide-carts'. These, he said, were thought to have been parallel poles with a platform in between. The ends of the poles would have been 'shod' with stone, thus wearing the grooves through constant use; but nobody had ever discovered just what method of traction had been used.

'They're all over the island,' he told Libby, pouring more wine into her glass. 'Sometimes there are so many that they look like a railway siding—one group's even called Clapham Junction. Nothing like them has ever been found anywhere else in the world, so whatever method of transport the Bronze Age Maltese had evolved, it was something nobody else thought of. Or perhaps the peculiar geology of Malta has preserved the ruts for us to see, where in other countries they've simply worn away or been buried. Malta is mostly rock, with just a thin covering of soil, and most of that has eroded over the centuries.'

Libby listened, fascinated. If only Keir would go on talking like this. It gave her a chance to get accustomed to being with him again, without having to worry about her emotions—and his. But she couldn't avoid the look in his eyes, even when he was talking about the history that was at present his main interest. It was a hungry look, full of yearning, and it set up a responsive hunger in herself. It wouldn't take too much to make her give in—and that, she knew, could be disastrous.

Libby was already beginning to recognise that the danger was greater than she had supposed. She was all too likely to give in to Keir—but she knew that by doing so she would be risking any peace of mind she might have for the rest of her life. For once she allowed Keir to love her as he wanted to, she would be totally and irrevocably committed; whether or not he regained his memory, and whatever he might feel about her if he did.

They were having breakfast on the balcony next morning when Jeremy Brooke arrived. He came in without knocking, breezing through the living-room to the balcony and greeting Libby with a cheerful smile before helping himself to coffee. He didn't seem a bit surprised to see her, she thought, but then Keir had probably confided in him. Maybe he'd kept out of the way for the past two days from a sense of delicacy—though he didn't look the sensitive type, with his shaggy brown beard and his bluff, hearty manner.

'This is Libby,' Keir said, introducing them. 'She's decided to stay on for a while—help us with the research.'

'My side or yours?' Jeremy asked, and Libby noticed that he had bright, twinkling brown eyes. 'Don't say I'm to have company in my stuffy archives!'

'No, you're not,' Keir told him bluntly. 'You just keep your head down amongst the documents, Jeremy. Libby's going to tag around with me and see the sights. But I might let you come with us sometimes, just for a change of scene.'

He broke off another piece of bread from the flat round loaf he had collected from somewhere in the village that morning. 'As a matter of fact, you can have Libby's company this morning if you like—I want to write up some notes. Then you can come back here for lunch and a siesta, and we could all go to Rabat this evening. Have a meal in Mdina, perhaps.'

'Can't manage that,' Jeremy said ruefully. 'I've got a date with that man at the Grand Master's Palace. But I'll be happy to entertain Libby this morning.' He gave Libby a bow and she couldn't help smiling back. Jeremy Brooke, she thought, would be a very easy man to like.

'Oh, please,' she said quickly, 'you don't have to feel you need to entertain me. I'm quite happy to potter around on my own. I'll have a look around Zurrieq, and perhaps—'

'Any pottering around you're doing will be done with me,' Jeremy told her firmly, sounding like an A. A. Milne poem Libby vaguely remembered from her childhood. What was it? *You must never go down to the end of the town, if you don't go down with me*. She smiled at the thought, then looked up and caught Jeremy's bright eyes twinkling at her. 'We'll go and see the Blue Grotto,' he went on persuasively. 'Keir will never take you there, it's nothing to do with his history of Malta, and it's full of trippers. But very pretty all the same.'

'All right,' Libby agreed, and as soon as they had all finished breakfast she went to her room and changed from her shorts and T-shirt to a full blue skirt with a yellow sleeveless blouse. She brushed her short dark hair into a cap of feathers, touched her eyelids with a silvery eyeshadow that brought out the clear grey of her eyes, and added a flick of pink lipstick and a dab of flowery perfume.

'Very nice too,' Jeremy approved as he led her out to his car. 'Afraid I don't have a very grand carriage. Nine-tenths of the hire-cars on Malta look as if they've been on one of these moto-cross rallies. Battered but willing, that's the best you can say of them. But I don't think it will actually fall apart on us, so if you're willing to risk yourself in it . . .'

'If it'll carry you, I'm sure it will carry me,' Libby said with a glance at his huge figure, which seemed to have been built on a pattern more usually reserved for grizzly bears. She slid into the front seat and the whole car sighed and settled closer against the ground as Jeremy heaved himself in the other side.

'Well, it's not far down to Wied-iz-Zurrieq—that's the little harbour where the boats go from to the Blue Grotto. It *is* a bit tripperish, but not too bad—there's not much there to spoil! And the Grotto itself doesn't get crowded, only two or three boats can go in at a time.'

They drove out of the maze of streets that made up Zurrieq. Some of them were almost too tiny for the car to squeeze through, and Libby could see how hire-cars, driven by people unused to the twisting alleys, would soon achieve the battered look of the little car Jeremy referred to with wry affection as Beat-up Bertie. Negotiation of the narrow passages was complicated by Maltese drivers who did know their way and raced through with blithe disregard for other traffic, using bumpers and mudguards to shoulder a path through and overtaking, where there was room, on right or left as the mood took them.

'Why ever did they build the streets this narrow?' Libby asked as a lorry, painted bright blue, decorated with red and yellow scrolls and with the name of Our Lady of Sorrows in ornate script on its bonnet, missed them by inches. 'They must have had mule-carts, or donkeys—didn't they need just as much room for them?'

'Almost certainly, but remember that Malta's history has never been particularly peaceful. At the time of the Knights of St John there was always the chance of a Turkish invasion. The country villages weren't fortified, except for central towers like the one at Qrendi—that's the next village to Zurrieq, you'll have gone through it yesterday on your way to Hagar Qim—so the intricate maze of narrow streets was a fortification in itself. The locals could confuse and baffle an invading army, lead it into dead-ends or round in circles, then attack it from the roof-tops. Simple and effective—and they didn't have to worry about traffic-jams in those days.'

They had left the village behind now and were driving along a cliff-road that wound along the side of the valley visible from Keir's flat. Libby twisted in her seat to look back, wondering if he might be watching them, but she couldn't be sure which was the right building and she turned her attention instead to the increasingly beautiful views as the road ran above the sapphire sea and the cliffs twisted themselves into spectacular formations far below.

'Those are the Blue Grotto caves,' Jeremy told her, stopping the car so that she could take in the incredible view. 'See, there's a boat going round now—they go back and forth all day, when it's calm. This is the best time of day to see the caves too, when the sun's on them. They really are worth seeing. Malta's claims to natural beauty aren't very great, in my opinion—too stark and bare, I like some trees and greenery myself—but the Blue Grotto really is something.'

They continued on down the steep, winding road to the little harbour of Wied-iz-Zurrieq and Jeremy parked the car. It was a colourful scene—just enough tourists to bring life to the minute village—and the inlet itself was more like a fiord running into the steep valley, its tossing waters bright with the gaily-painted boats that waited to take visitors to the caves. Libby followed Jeremy down the rocky steps and into a boat with half a dozen other people, all festooned with cameras. Libby felt regretful at not having brought her own, but she just hadn't thought to pack it. When she had answered Keir's letter, she hadn't looked on her trip to Malta as a holiday.

Her mind went back to Keir as the little boat set off, leaving the shelter of the harbour for the open sea that surrounded Malta, washing endlessly in a blue and white spray against the foot of the towering white cliffs. No wonder Malta had been a fortress for so many different warrior nations, she thought, craning her neck to see to the top, where cars drove like miniature toys along the road from Zurrieq. From this coast, at least, it was impregnable.

But was anything truly impregnable? For two years, knowing that she had sent Keir away, killed his love for her with the bitterness she had allowed to come between them, she had thought that his heart too was an impregnable fortress—at least, to her. And now he had sent for her, he wanted her again. What did it mean?

Should she take what Keir had offered her—his heart and his love on the old terms? Heaven knew, she wanted to! And there was, surely, every chance that he was right in saying that what he felt for her must be real, whatever had happened since. Even if—when—he did remember the past two years, he believed he would still feel the same for her. So couldn't she accept that and take the risk?

Libby turned her head and looked at Jeremy, his big bear's head warm and shaggy against the harshness of the rocks. Perhaps he could help her. She didn't know how long he had known Keir, but it had certainly been since before the accident. So wouldn't he be able to answer some of her questions?

Before she could speak, the Maltese guide at the helm of the little boat began to tell them about the cliffs and the caves, and the other tourists began to crane their necks and take photographs. In any case, she told herself, this was neither the time nor the place to begin questioning Jeremy; it would be better left until they were ashore again and could talk privately, perhaps over a coffee or cool drink. And it would be churlish, when Jeremy had given up his morning to bring her here, not to show pleasure and interest in what he clearly considered beautiful.

And it *was* beautiful—there was no doubt at all about that. The warm air caressed Libby's cheek and bare arms as the boat crept closer to the cliffs which reared like solid grey walls above them. Great spurs of rock curved out like the paws of a gigantic lion, toes dipped in the clear blue sea which moved on a gentle swell underneath them. And, as the boat drew closer; Libby could see the dark mouths of the caves themselves, cool and mysterious.

'Look into the water,' Jeremy murmured as they floated slowly into the dome of one of the caverns—not huge, not intimidating, but strange and almost unearthly, its curving roof lit by the blue reflection of the water. 'See the sponges? Just outside, in the sunlight, you can see all their different colours. And here—dip your hand in the water and see what happens.'

Curiously, Libby did so, and uttered a squeak as her hand turned an almost fluorescent blue under the water. Fascinated, she dipped a little further, watching the same colour stain her slender arm; then she withdrew it, half relieved to find her skin its normal colour while sparkling drops fell back into the dancing waves.

The boat came back out into the sunlight. Other boats followed as they explored the rest of the caves and then turned to go back to the harbour. Libby sat back in her seat, glad to have seen the beauty of the caves, and grateful to Jeremy for bringing her. Grateful, too, for the fact that she now knew the big researcher a little better and felt easy about asking him her questions. After all, she had a right to the answers—hadn't she?

'Well, yes, I do agree that you have a right to know what's been happening—up to a point.' Jeremy poured Libby a glass of fresh, iced orange juice from the jug between them. But he didn't look directly at her; his glance was directed towards the sea from the little clifftop café where they were sitting, and Libby was disconcerted to see that he was frowning slightly, as if unsure what to say.

'Up to a point? What do you mean?' Libby's voice was edged with anxiety. 'Jeremy, I'm in an impossible situation—I'm no better off than Keir himself. All *he* remembers is what happened between us two years ago—and that's all *I* know, too! Surely it would be better if I had *some* idea what's been happening in that time? And you're the best one to tell me.'

'That's true enough,' he agreed. 'I've been with Keir for practically all that time, acting as researcher and general assistant. And I've enjoyed it a lot. Got to know Keir pretty well, too. But I'm not sure about telling you—I'm not even sure what you want to know.'

Libby was silent. She sipped her orange juice, wondering how to put it. *She* knew well enough what she was really asking—and she had hoped that, as Jeremy told her other things, her own specific questions would be answered along the way. But it didn't look as if Jeremy were going to talk quite so readily. And she didn't feel able to put her question quite so baldly. After all, how *could* she ask Keir's researcher and friend just what women there'd been in Keir's life? And that was what she really wanted to know.

Instead, she shrugged as if she wasn't too sure herself. 'Oh, you know, general things,' she said vaguely. 'Anything you might think could help, I suppose. What he's been doing, where he's been going, all that kind of thing.'

'Mm.' Jeremy gave her a bright glance and she wondered uneasily whether he understood her better than he pretended. 'But I'm not sure it's really going to help you much, you know. After all, you haven't seen or even had much contact with Keir in that time, unless I'm mistaken.' His glance was frankly enquiring now, and Libby felt her colour rise as she shook her head. 'So you can't really remind him of any events or incidents. You can't jog that memory of his. And anything I can tell you might even make things worse—colour your own attitude in some way.'

And that could only mean other women, Libby thought. Jeremy believed that if she knew the truth about what had been happening to Keir during their separation she would leave him. It was as easy as that. And—following on from that—if he didn't want to tell her, it must mean that he didn't want her to leave. Why?

'Can't you just tell me about the accident?' she asked desperately. 'If I knew *something*—I just feel lost about the whole thing, Jeremy.'

Jeremy gave her a long look. 'Yes, I can see it's awkward,' he said. 'Not an easy position for you at all, is it? Forgive me if I seem over-protective—it's just that I look up to Keir and it was pretty ghastly when he first came round and didn't know who he was. Like watching a grown man suddenly revert to babyhood. I suppose I have tended to look after him a bit since then—though I'd never dream of letting him know it. And I've been especially careful to see that he doesn't have any more problems. He was pretty shaken when your letter came, and nobody else knew he'd written to you—yes, he told me about that this morning, while you were getting changed. So I wanted to be sure you wouldn't hurt him.'

'And that's why you took the morning off to take me to the Blue Grotto,' Libby exclaimed, and he grinned apologetically.

'Afraid so. Not that I often pass up the chance to take out a pretty girl! But I did want a chance to get to know you on my own—make my own judgment, if you like, though I feel a bit mean admitting it.'

'And?' Libby said quietly, meeting his eyes.

'And I think you deserve to know a little at least of what you're asking. Later on, perhaps I'll tell you more.

But I meant what I said, Libby—I honestly don't think it would help either of you to know too much, not at this stage. That's why I haven't even told Keir very much. When he remembers, he's got to remember on his own—not persuade himself that he recalls things someone else has told him.'

Libby digested his words and had to admit that there was sense in them. And hadn't Keir said much the same thing at some stage? What he wanted from her seemed to be mostly reassurance that the memories he did have were true ones. That's why he had continually talked about their engagement. That and a natural desire to convince himself that their love was still real, still existed.

Well, that was something neither of them could know for certain until he remembered the rest. Meanwhile, in spite of the common sense behind Jeremy's words, Libby still had an intense curiosity about Keir's forgotten life; and she was still determined to find out as much as she could—whether from Jeremy Brooke, or from others who might be persuaded to talk to her. Though who they might be, she had at present no idea at all.

She looked up at Jeremy and her eyes were wide and limpid, like crystal pools.

'Go on, then,' she said. 'Tell me, tell me whatever you can about Keir's accident, and about what else has happened to him.'

CHAPTER FIVE

THE town of Rabat was alive with people in the warm evening air, and Libby wandered at Keir's side, fascinated by the street market and the strange cries of the vendors calling for people to buy their fish, fruit and other wares. Their dark eyes were eager, darting this way and that as they looked for custom, and they quickly recognised Libby as a stranger who might well be persuaded to buy. A fractional pause by a stall selling highly-coloured cream cakes had the man wielding a huge knife to cut a sample off, but Libby hastily shook her head. Previous experience had taught her that such samples were by no means 'without obligation' and that having accepted one it was difficult to walk away without buying. In any case, the bright colours of the cream attracted her only as a spectacle; her taste didn't run to such rich confections.

All the shops were open as well, and Libby's eye was caught, as they explored the winding streets, by doorways that led into caverns filled with a mixture of goods. There were few shop windows, and it was sometimes difficult to decide which doors belonged to shops and which to private houses; pulling aside one cane curtain she found herself staring in at a Maltese family meal, and hastily drew back. Keir chuckled as he led her away and Libby was glad that it was too dark for him to see how embarrassed she was.

'It's quite different here from in Valletta,' she remarked. 'Valletta is more cosmopolitan—this seems to be real Maltese.'

'Mm. In fact it was originally a suburb of Mdina—that's what its name means. It's an interesting old place—I'll bring you to see the catacombs one day. That's the ancient Christian burial place, and they're very extensive. They were used as shelters during the war.'

He took her arm, and Libby felt a shock jar through her as his fingers brushed the thin cotton of her dress. She bit her lip, hoping that the sensation hadn't been powerful enough to transfer itself to him. Since Jeremy's revelations that afternoon, she had made up her mind that the only way she could survive this was to play it cool—very cool indeed.

Jeremy hadn't meant to tell her so much, of course. He'd made that clear from the beginning. But once he had begun, telling her about the accident that had landed Keir in hospital, it had been quite easy to encourage him to go on. He clearly thought a lot of Keir and was only too pleased to talk about the places they had visited to research Keir's books, the people they had met and the friends they had made. And from that point, it was almost impossible for him not to mention the women.

Libby pulled her mind back to the present. Keir was leading her away now from the hubbub of Rabat and across a deep, dry moat. Looking up, she could see the floodlit triumphal gateway with its carved arch and rampant beasts guarding the entrance to the city. Then they passed through and Libby was instantly conscious of the contrast.

Outside, it was all noise and bustle, humanity at its most gregarious. In here, there was tranquillity and peace, a quietness that pervaded the air so that even the people walking through the narrow streets and tiny squares spoke in lowered voices. There were few cars—

Keir had told her that they used to be banned altogether—and the tiny city seemed to be a world alone, isolated from the boisterous hurrying of the rest of the island.

'The Silent City,' Keir said as if echoing her thoughts. 'It's really more truly Maltese than anywhere else on the island—it was here that the aristocracy of the island drew together, uninfluenced by the Knights of St John who ruled.' He led her through the streets between tall, dignified houses and *palazzi*. 'In some ways, it's a museum in itself—but it's still very much alive.' He indicated a shop selling leather and suede goods, and another displaying exquisite lace. 'You come here for quality—they'll make you a suit in suede, and if you can't collect it they'll send it to England for you.' They walked on through the quiet passages. 'Come and look at the view from the walls. It's best at sunset, when everything glows with pink, but we're too late for that today. We'll come again to see it.'

Libby followed him up on the walls and looked across the island. It was dark enough now to see the great bowl of the sky, spattered with stars, and it was almost impossible, as she looked out, to tell which of the sparkling lights were stars and which were earth-bound. A great cluster not far away belonged to Mosta, Keir said, and he told her the story of the bomb that had fallen into the cathedral during a service, bouncing against the walls as it dropped from the huge dome, and coming to rest in front of the terrified congregation without exploding. It was still there, in a small room, and was one of the attractions of the church.

Libby stood beside him, shivering slightly in the breeze that found its way across the rocky plain, and wondered if he'd brought any other woman to this point. She felt his hand resting lightly on her shoulder, and a tingle ran through her body as his fingertips caressed her bare arm. Play it cool, she remembered, play it cool. There was only pain in store if she let her heart rule her head. And although she wanted nothing more than to move closer to the warmth of his lean body, to rest against his hard strength, she moved away so that his hand could no longer reach her skin.

'I'm getting hungry,' she murmured, though food had been furthest from her thoughts, and Keir nodded and turned away at once.

'Then we'll eat. There are several very good restaurants in the city, so we won't have to walk far. We must come here again during the day—there are quite a lot of things to see. The Magisterial Palace—it's a Natural History museum now—the cathederal and its museum, and several smaller churches. And just outside the gate is a Roman villa, together with its own museum, of course! The Maltese seem to love them, but then they have a lot of history to display.'

He took Libby into a dimly-lit restaurant and they were shown to a table by a long window, looking out on a courtyard with a single fig tree growing in the middle. The walls were decorated with pieces of armour and old weapons, and candles flickered in glasses on the dark wood of the tables.

The meal took a long time and Libby was happy to linger over every delicious mouthful. She was already beginning to feel tinglingly nervous about their return to the flat. It wasn't at all wise, she was sure, for her to go on staying there alone with Keir. All right, he'd made a promise, but it was quite clearly one he didn't want to keep and although he'd shown iron control during their engagement it didn't mean he'd do the same now. And Libby was uncomfortably aware that her own control had never been that good—she had longed for Keir to love her from the start, and now that she was with him again after such a long separation, she felt her yearnings as a continual ache.

Savouring the taste of the *timpana* Keir had chosen for her, Libby thought back to Jeremy's story that morning. He hadn't told her everything, she knew, but he'd let slip far more than he had intended to. And that was just what Libby *had* intended, but afterwards she wasn't sure that having her suspicions confirmed had helped her at all. So now she knew that Keir had had plenty of girl-friends during those two years—did it make things any better? Or worse? Or did it just not make any difference at all?

'Enjoying it?' Keir asked, breaking in on her thoughts, and she felt herself blush as she looked up with a start. 'The *timpana*,' he added patiently. 'Is it good?'

'Oh—oh, yes, it's splendid. It seems to have just about everything in it.' She touched the delicate flaky pastry with her fork.

'It has, almost. Cheese, minced meat, aubergines, onions, eggs, tomato—it's quite a mixture. Tasty, though.'

'Mm, it certainly is.' Libby finished and laid her knife and fork on the empty plate. 'I'm not sure if I can manage a dessert.'

'Oh, I'm sure you can. They specialise in a particularly delicious concoction called *prinjolata* here—a sort of pyramid of sponge fingers filled with almonds and cream and covered with melted chocolate and cherries. It's a carnival dish, but they know the tourists will eat it at any time.'

'I really don't think I could—' Libby began, but Keir gave the order anyway, remarking that what she couldn't eat he certainly could, and Libby subsided. It would be nice to try it anyway—and when it came she found it was so featherlight that she could eat almost the whole portion, thus thwarting Keir's plan to have two helpings.

'That really was delicious,' Libby said as they emerged at last into the quiet, moonlit streets. 'And I love the Marsala we drank with it. You're spoiling me, Keir—tomorrow I really must do some work and earn my living.'

'Must you? Why?' Keir's voice was soft and deep as he led her up a short flight of steps to lean against the ancient wall and look out across the darkened plain. 'If you were my wife now, you'd be doing just what you are doing—accompanying me, helping me, just being with me. And as far as I'm concerned, that's what you should be—my wife.' He drew her close and Libby could feel her heart thump against his. 'Don't hold back, Libby. Don't pretend we're strangers—we're not. This is the way we're meant to be—can't you feel it? Can't you see what you're doing to me—to us?' His fingers were hard, almost cruel, on her soft arms.

'We've wasted enough time, Libby. God knows why, but could there really have been any reason for us to stay apart for two years? Don't let's waste any more.' His lips were on hers before she could begin to reply, and her swift protest died before it could be voiced as his mouth made demands that were impossible to refuse. She felt her mouth open under his, felt the sweetness as his tongue met hers and his teeth made tiny nips at the soft flesh of her lips, felt the inevitable weakness as his strength overcame her feeble efforts to struggle. Then, knowing just what she did but not caring any more, she let her hands move of their own accord, wound her arms round his neck, tangled her fingers in his thick hair and shaped her palm around the nape of his neck, returning his kiss and pressing her body close against his in passionate response.

Keir made a tiny sound of triumph and dragged his mouth away from hers and down the slender column of her neck, as far as the low scoop of her blouse. Her heart leapt under his kiss and instinctively she tilted her head back, arching her breasts towards him in open invitation, moving sensuously as his fingers pulled the elasticated neck lower to make way for his seeking lips. Their warmth was like fire on her cool skin, sending shudders of delight through her body, and the blood pulsed through her veins in intoxicating rhythm, making a music of her desire, a song of yearning and love.

'We're not strangers,' Keir muttered against her breast. 'Why pretend we are? Why worry about the future—it may never happen. Let's take what we've got now, Libby, take it and enjoy it. Hold me—ah, hold me, my sweet, and never let me go again.'

Dazed, Libby clung to him, every nerve in her body focused on his touch. His words washed over her, barely heard; yet even after his murmurings had ceased she could still vaguely hear them, lingering in her ears. Strangers . . . the future . . . Her mind struggled for attention, but the clamour of her body was more powerful as Keir's caresses became more intimate, more demanding, and Libby moaned faintly and moved against him. Strangers . . . what had he said about their being strangers? Treating each other as strangers, that was it, starting from the beginning, but what Keir was doing now wasn't any sort of beginning and she almost cried out at the sharp delight of it. And the future . . . had she been worrying about it, about what would happen to her if Keir regained his memory—and didn't love her after all? Oh Keir, Keir, she begged silently, don't stop loving me, don't stop . . . But she knew she must stop him before he went too far. He wouldn't, surely, in this place which, although it was a hidden corner was still a public place . . .

Suddenly panic-stricken, she wriggled in his arms, trying to escape, but Keir only held her more tightly and she knew that her struggles were having no effect, were only stimulating a passion that had almost taken him over—had almost taken them both over . . . With a last surge of effort, she twisted away from him, using elbows and hands to push herself away from that warm, magnetic body, and half fell down the steps into the road.

'Libby! What the hell—?' Keir stumbled, then regained his balance and stood staring down at her from the wall. 'What's the matter? No one will see us there.'

'I don't care whether they can or not!' Libby panted. 'Keir, you *promised*—I thought I was safe. We agreed, didn't we, to take it slowly, to start from the beginning, get to know each other all over again. That was the only reason I stayed. And if you won't keep that promise—' her voice shook. '—I won't be *able* to stay. I'll have to go back to England. Don't you understand?'

Keir came down the steps, pushing strong fingers through the thick corn of his hair. 'Hell, I know we agreed, Libby, but it was crazy, we *aren't* strangers, we *do* know each other. And we *want* each other—you can't fool me, or even yourself, about *that*. We're not children, Libby. We're adults, and when two adults love each other and need each other like we do, well, there's only one conclusion. You can't escape that.'

Libby stared at him in the darkness. She could see the gleam of his teeth as he spoke, the glitter of his eyes; the bulk of him made a dark shape against the moon-bright sky. She wanted nothing more than to be folded against that tall, firm body—but it wouldn't do. To Keir, the future might seem simple and clear-cut, but Libby had been hurt once already and she just wasn't prepared to risk it again.

Keir had been hurt too, she thought wryly, but he didn't remember it. When he did, it might not be just another woman who stood between them. It might well be his memories of Libby herself.

'Please, Keir,' she said in a low voice. 'Let's stick to our agreement. Don't go too quickly. I just can't cope with it.'

Keir stared at her for a long moment, his face shadowed. Then he shrugged lightly and turned away a little, sending a pang of fear through Libby's heart. Surely he wasn't going to give up too easily! And then she chided herself for being inconsistent—did she want Keir to keep his promise, or didn't she?

Keir was walking slowly along the road now, and Libby fell into step beside him. For a few minutes neither of them spoke; then, just as Libby was about to speak, Keir's voice sounded, harsh and blank.

'I suppose you've been pretty busy during the past two years. Got on well with the job? Lots of boy-friends?'

'Yes, the job's going quite well,' Libby said quietly. 'And no, not many boy-friends.'

'Just the one special one, perhaps.' Keir spoke almost indifferently, glancing up at the walls that towered on either side of them, but Libby gave him a quick glance. Surely he didn't think *that* was why she . . . ? But he wouldn't admit it if he did.

'No, not even a special one,' she answered lightly, and thought of Terry, who had wanted to be special. And might have been, if she hadn't fallen in love with Keir first. Even now, he didn't really know . . . She made up her mind that she must write to Terry as soon as possible, tell him there was no point in waiting for her.

Wasn't there? And why not? Because there really might be a future with Keir?

Or because there was no future for her with anyone else?

They walked back through the Silent City, their footsteps loud in the quiet streets. Not many people were about now and the tall buildings loomed towards the sky, making the narrow passages dark except where the moon was able to send its rays through the spreading roofs. Libby wondered what kind of people lived here now. There was a nunnery, she knew, where the nuns lived in such strict seclusion that the only men allowed in were the doctor and the whitewasher. An odd combination, and Libby thought it was strange that a whitewasher should be deemed so important.

What was it like to live in such a closed community, she wondered. What had the lives of the women been before they became nuns? Did they miss the company of men at all? Or were they glad to be done with the complications of relationships with the other sex? Were they relieved to have finished with the complexities of love, or did they sometimes long for something earthier than prayer?

Keir took her back across the dry moat to the car, and Libby got in. Rabat itself was quieter now, the shops closed at last and only a few people still in the streets. She sat without speaking as Keir drove along the twisting roads back to Zurrieq; and as they approached the village she felt her nervousness return. Had he accepted her ultimatum, or would he try yet again to persuade her? She was tinglingly aware that her defences were too weak to withstand another onslaught, and she was pretty sure that Keir knew it. Would he take advantage of the power he had over her, or would he respect her wish to go more slowly? If he were really sure of himself, she thought fatalistically, he'd do just that. Because he must know that he would win in the end.

She shifted restlessly in her seat as the car purred through the moonlit lanes, passing the rubble walls that lined every tiny, terraced field on the island. Didn't what Jeremy had told her this afternoon make any difference at all? Didn't it affect her feelings to know just what had been going on during those past two years?

'I suppose it was when we were in Rome that things began to get serious,' Jeremy had said, talking almost as if to himself as he stared out at the sea. 'Before that, there'd been women of course—Keir's not the man to go without women for long—but nothing serious, nothing that lasted. And then, while we were in Rome, he met this *contessa*. I can't remember all her name—it was one of those long jobs that sound like the title of an opera—but that didn't matter because he called her Pia, and so did I after a while. She was always around, you see; where Keir was, so was she. She lived in a *palazzo* in a quiet part of the city; a big, crumbling place, but magnificent inside. It wasn't long before she persuaded Keir to move in there, and—'

'You mean they lived together?' Libby broke in, and Jeremy looked round at her, startled. For a second he hesitated, evidently remembering that he hadn't intended telling her any of this, then he shrugged slightly and went on.

'I don't know that they actually *lived* together,' he said, frowning. 'Not in the sense you mean. I moved in too, and I certainly didn't "live" with the *contessa*. But it was a huge place—you needed a map to find your way round it—and I never knew quite where the *contessa* had her private rooms. I knew where Keir's were, of course, but they were quite a distance from mine.'

And it was easy enough to guess why, Libby thought.

The *contessa* knew her way around her own *palazzo* well enough, and no doubt her own rooms were near enough to Keir's, with Jeremy kept at a respectable distance, too far away to hear any sounds that might be made in the night. A cold hand seemed to clutch at her heart as she thought of Keir and his *contessa*, sharing the *palazzo* in Rome; making love amongst the decaying splendour to the sound of fountains in the courtyard and the sighing of the soft wind in the pines . . . She shook herself angrily. She had *known* Keir would have had other women during their separation. There had been no reason, no reason at all why he shouldn't—their engagement was off, all ties had been snapped. So why should she feel so hurt; and why so frightened?

Because this one was serious, a voice whispered in her head. Because he might still be in love with his *contessa*.

'How—how long ago was this?' she asked through a dry throat.

Jeremy sighed. 'I wish I'd never started to tell you. I don't even know how I did. But since I've said so much—well, it started about nine or ten months ago.'

'And finished?'

'That's just it,' Jeremy said miserably. 'I can't tell you when it finished. I don't even know for sure that it has.'

Libby stared at him. 'You—you mean this affair could still be going on? But you've been with Keir all that time. Surely you've some idea—surely you know when he last saw her.'

'Not absolutely, no. You see, I left Keir in Italy and went to London for about three or four weeks—that was, let's see, just over three months ago. Then I came directly to Malta and got this flat organised before Keir joined me. All I know is that Pia hasn't been to Malta—as far as I know. But that could mean anything—or nothing.'

'But what about his accident? Wouldn't she have come then? Did anyone let her know?'

'No—I was the only one who could have done that, and I didn't know where to contact her. I didn't even know if I should—Keir could have broken with her, not want to see her. He doesn't always confide in me, you know. Why should he? I'm just his researcher—'

'And his friend,' Libby interrupted swiftly.

'Yes, I like to think so. But that doesn't mean he's got to tell me all the details of his private life. Anyway, I had no address for Pia, all I knew was that she had intended closing the *palazzo* for a few months and going away. I didn't know where—I assumed to be with Keir until he came here alone. I never asked him, and he never told me where she was going or why. And then when I realised he didn't remember—well, it was difficult to know what to do. I just thought it was best to let things ride, and he seemed to agree with me, that was until you arrived on the scene.'

'And he remembers nothing about her?' Libby said wonderingly.

'Nothing. She belongs entirely to the blank patch in his life.'

Libby heaved a sigh. How complicated it all was! There was no way of knowing what the situation had been between Keir and Pia before his accident. Only Pia knew, and nobody knew where she was.

'I think he must have broken with her, you know,' Jeremy was saying anxiously. 'Or she would have come, surely. Even if she hadn't heard about his accident, she would have been here by now.'

'Yes, I suppose so.' But Libby didn't feel at all sure. There were a hundred reasons why Pia might not have come to Keir yet. And not all of them meant a break-up in the affair.

There was no point in worrying about it, she knew. But until she could be sure that Pia no longer took first place in Keir's heart, she could not abandon herself to his love as he so urgently wanted her to. The *contessa* would always stand between them until she could be certain, one way or the other.

And at the present rate of progress that might be never.

They arrived at the flat in silence and Libby followed Keir inside, her heart quaking. But he did not seem inclined to touch her again, or even to speak. He walked over to the big window and stood with his back to the room, staring out into the darkness.

Libby had a sudden searing vision of what this situation must be like for him. The past weeks must have been a long passage of bewilderment, first of all knowing nothing at all, a mind as fresh as that of a baby; then the slow awakening of the reflexes, the things that had been known for so long that they were indelibly imprinted on the brain—language, recognition of all the things needed for survival. And the realisation that there ought to be more even than this, that there were names he ought to be able to remember, including his own, faces that he should know.

It must have been like a nightmare. And the more he remembered, the more nightmarish it would become—because as he remembered more he would become increasingly aware of the things he *couldn't* remember. Libby shuddered. It was almost too horrible to think about.

And then he had remembered her. Remembered their love, the happiness they had shared. No wonder he had written her that letter, begging her to come to him—even if, later, he had forgotten doing it, even if he had realised the bleak truth that too much time had passed for their relationship to have remained the same; that something must have gone wrong in the time between his last clear memory and now.

But Libby had answered his letter. She had come to him. And nothing was the same. Or—no, that wasn't true. The passion, the desire that flared between them was the same, it was stronger than ever. But the happy, loving companionship that had been such a valuable part of their relationship—that had gone. Gone, perhaps, for ever—how could she tell? All she knew was that at that moment she felt an overwhelming pity for the lonely man who stood quite still, his back to her, staring out into the darkness of the Maltese night.

Silently, Libby turned and left the room.

The next few days passed slowly. Keir and Libby treated each other with a wary politeness that seemed to stretch Libby's nerves to a thin tautness that must surely give way. She wanted desperately to break through the barrier Keir seemed to have erected around himself, but each time she tried he looked at her with a remote, mocking glance that had her scarlet with confusion. Make up your mind, he seemed to be saying, one way or the other. You can't have it both ways. Either you love me and we go ahead from there, or we remain strangers. It can't be both.

Libby wanted to tell him that she didn't want to be strangers, but she knew that if she did he would want more than she could give at the moment. So she would retreat behind her own barrier, polite but distant, and wonder miserably when the nightmare would end.

It was this barrier that had prevented her from approaching him on the night of their visit to Mdina. She had stood there, looking at his rigid back with a yearning hunger, longing to go to him, throw her arms around him, draw his head down to her breast. But it would only have made things worse. His passion, so near the surface that it was almost violence, would have overwhelmed them both. And if he had realised that it was pity that had brought her to him, it would have been replaced by anger.

Libby wondered several times why she didn't simply pack up and go home. There seemed to be so little point in her staying. But somehow, she could not bring herself to leave Keir; deep down she still had the feeling that he needed her. At any moment, he might remember those lost years and she would know the truth. She could not go back to London while everything was still so undecided.

In spite of the tension between them, Libby found herself unexpectedly enjoying herself as Keir took her around the island, showing her the historical sites and explaining their place in the island's culture. Acting as his assistant, helping him to make notes and sort them into some kind of order in the evenings, Libby felt at least that she was being of some help. And she enjoyed the times when Jeremy joined them and told them about his own researches. The book was beginning to take shape under their discussions and Libby was beginning to feel a proprietorial interest in it.

It was on the fourth night, as Jeremy left and Libby began to tidy up the papers that they had strewn all over the room, that Keir came back and she felt a change in the atmosphere; an electricity almost like that of an impending thunderstorm. Slowly, she straightened and met his eyes.

Keir was standing at the door, lounging against the wall, but his body was about as relaxed as a tiger's when it scents its prey. His eyes, dark as the night outside, seemed to be nailing Libby to the floor; she had a feeling that if she tried to move her muscles wouldn't obey her. Even her chest felt tight and her gasp was stifled as her heart lurched violently against her ribs.

'Keir?' she breathed, but the sound was almost inaudible, and when he lifted himself from the wall and moved towards her she found herself mesmerised, unable either to move or to speak.

Keir's advance seemed almost to be in slow motion, but he finally reached her and took her arms in strong fingers, holding her with a firmness that would, with only a slight increase in pressure, become cruelty. Libby stared up at him, soft lips parted slightly as she begged him mutely to let her go; but if he understood the message of her frightened eyes, he ignored it.

Libby closed her eyes, knowing that there was nothing she could do to prevent the inevitable conclusion. Keir had waited long enough; she should have known that this would happen if she stayed here alone with him in his flat, knowing how he felt. It was her own fault. And she tilted her face towards his, closed her eyes and let her lips part in acceptance as she waited for his kiss.

But Keir's mouth did not touch hers. Instead, there was a long silence; and Libby opened her eyes to find him staring down at her with an expression she couldn't interpret.

'Keir?' she repeated uncomfortably. 'Keir, what is it?' A sudden panic hit her. 'Have—have you remembered?'

'About you and me? No—no more than I had before.' With an abrupt movement he dropped his hands and turned away from her. 'I wish I had! Then perhaps I'd be free—free of this torment, not knowing what the situation really is between us, not knowing what went wrong. All I do know is that I love you—I'd swear that that's true and nothing I remember will change it. And I'm just as certain that you love me. But there's this damned barrier between us, and nothing I do will break it down.'

Libby watched him, her eyes wide with distress. Keir was pacing the room now, his face thin and shadowed, his eyes haunted. More than ever, she wanted to go to him, take him in her arms, love him—but again, she knew that he wouldn't accept her love now until everything was clear between them.

Somehow or other we've changed places, she thought dully. But it was her heart that was talking now, not her head. In her mind, she knew that caution was still the best way. And it was her caution that had built this barrier that kept Keir away from her.

Libby sank into a chair and buried her face in her hands. Was there no way out of this impasse? No way they could find out the truth?

'Wouldn't it be better to talk about it?' she asked, her voice ragged. 'You don't have to go through life not knowing—not when others can tell you. Keir, wouldn't it be better for me to tell you about the way our engagement ended? Wouldn't it be better for Jeremy to tell you what he knows about the time you've forgotten?' And what I know too, she added silently. 'You're like a man in a dark room, refusing to have the light put on. It's crazy—it's driving *you* crazy.'

'You've got it wrong, Libby,' Keir said heavily. 'I'm not like a man in a darkened room. I'm like a *blind* man—no amount of lights switched on are going to make any difference to me. Try explaining light to a man who was born blind—he can't believe you because he can't have any idea what it's like. And I won't be able to believe what you say, because to me it's nothing to do with my life. Or, I might *believe* you, in my mind, but I won't be able to *feel* its truth. Can you understand that?'

Libby nodded hopelessly. 'So there's nothing anyone can do?'

'Nothing. The doctors say my memory will probably return, given time. And then again, it may not. Those two years might have been wiped out for ever.' He whipped round, fixing those brilliant eyes on her with a look that seemed to burn through to her heart. 'So why do we have to let them matter, Libby? As far as I'm concerned, that quarrel never happened. Can't you think that way, too?'

They were off again, going round the same old circle. Libby rubbed her face with a weary gesture. Then, slowly, she rose to her feet and faced him.

'All right, Keir,' she said quietly. 'We'll try it your way. We'll forget that there have been two years between that afternoon on Dartmoor and tonight. Let's pick up again from where we left off.' She stood before him, her arms at her sides, looking curiously vulnerable. 'You're right, Keir—I do still love you. And I want you—just as I wanted you that afternoon. So what are you waiting for?'

Keir stared at her, his face disbelieving, incredulous. Then, like the sun breaking through cloud, a look of pure joy lit the gaunt features and the years dropped away as he gathered Libby into his arms. Her heart leapt as she felt the impact of their bodies, and then she was swung up from the floor, her feet inches from the ground, as he carried her swiftly through to his own bedroom. He laid her on the bed and stood looking down at her, eyes smouldering, and a faint tremor running through his body.

'You're sure?' he muttered huskily, and Libby nodded.

Slowly, tenderly, Keir began to undress her. It didn't take long to unbutton her loose sundress and slip off the lacy bra and panties that were all she wore underneath it, but he lingered over every sensuous movement, and

Libby moved with his hands, softly and languorously. And then she was naked, lying on the deep red coverlet, her body smooth and slender and tanned to a soft golden brown against the rich colour.

'I've dreamed of this,' Keir said huskily. 'And you're just the way I dreamed . . . Libby, you don't know what I've been going through, what hell I've been in . . .'

His own undressing was much swifter, the clothes dropped carelessly to the floor, and then he was beside her on the bed, his skin deliciously cool against hers, the friction of the golden hairs that covered his chest intoxicatingly abrasive against her satin-smooth breasts. She felt his legs tangle with hers, their length curling around her thighs and calves, toes caressing her ankles with a sensuality that took her by surprise. At the same time his hands were exploring every curve, bringing to life sensations she half knew of, but had never experienced in her waking hours. And just as she felt that there was too much to cope with, that she must beg him to let at least a part of her body have a little peace, he completed the sweet torment by laying his mouth firmly on hers, so that all she was conscious of was the thundering of her heart, the singing of her blood and the knowledge that this was what her body had been waiting for, hungering for, and this was why no other man had ever been able to awaken her.

Keir slid both his arms beneath her and lifted her into a sitting position, where they clung to each other and rocked to and fro. He laid her down again and covered her with his body; then rolled on to his back, lifting Libby with him so that she looked down at his face. Their eyes opened and met, gravely but with perfect understanding, and she knew that nothing could now come between them and the completion of their love, whatever the future might bring.

And then, just as Keir's look had changed to one of enquiry and Libby's eyes were answering him yes, *yes*, don't wait a second longer, the world was split by the angry shriek of the telephone. It shrilled in Libby's ear, sending her with a violent jerk to the other side of the bed, wrenching her out of Keir's arms in her shock and sending a wave of sudden and unreasonable terror through her mind.

'Don't listen to it,' Keir panted, reaching for her again. 'Don't listen to it, Libby—ah, come back to me, my sweet, come back—'

But the telephone would not be silenced. On and on, it shrilled, and the moment was shattered. Libby lay in Keir's arms, still breathing quickly, wanting desperately to feel again the soaring delight that seemed to have deserted her. Tentatively, she ran her hand down his back and felt him shiver; but still the shrieking continued and, with a sigh, Keir rolled over and lifted the receiver.

'Yes,' he said curtly, and Libby wondered who it could be, ringing so late at night. 'Yes, this is Keir Salinger. Who is that? I'm sorry, I don't re—I *beg* your pardon? You're—who? And you say— But I don't— Look, listen a moment, I— Hullo? Hullo?' He waited a moment, his face a mixture of emotions, then he thrust the receiver back on to its rest and turned to Libby, his face and eyes blank.

'That was a woman,' he said tonelessly. 'She says she knows me. She says she's coming here—soon—to see me. She seems to think I'll welcome her.' He paused and Libby watched his face, feeling suddenly afraid. 'She says her name is Pia.'

CHAPTER SIX

'PIA!'

Libby stared at him, shock freezing her body as she lay, half-raised on one elbow, on the tumbled bed. Pia—the Italian *contessa*—coming *here*, to Malta, to see Keir! What did it mean? And how was it going to affect her future—her future with Keir?

But did she *have* any future with Keir? With a thrill of dismay, she realised just what had been happening—had been about to happen. If Pia's telephone call hadn't come at just that moment, she would have been irrevocably committed to Keir—and he? Would he have been equally committed to her? Oh, he would have said so, no doubt, and believed it, too, but when he saw Pia again, what then? Would the memory of those months spent with the Italian woman have returned to him, and would he have realised that she was the woman he loved, and not Libby at all?

Oh God, what a mess! The thoughts ran through Libby's brain like frightened ants, searching for home and finding only dead-ends, with no conclusion, no safety. She rubbed a cold hand over her face and realised suddenly that she was still naked—and that Keir was watching her, his eyes dark with newly-dawning passion.

No! With a quick squirm of her slim body, Libby scrambled off the bed and grabbed the first thing that came to hand, which happened to be Keir's navy towelling robe. She wrapped it round her, hiding her trembling body from that scorching gaze, and backed away towards the door.

'Libby?' Keir's voice caught her before she could escape, its deep roughness stopping her in her tracks. 'Libby, where are you going? What is it?'

'Where am I going?' she gasped. 'Back to my own room, of course—where else? You can't expect me to . . .'

Keir was off the bed with a swing of long, muscular legs and Libby fumbled for the door, terror shuddering through her body. But he was too quick for her; one powerful hand closed around both her wrists and the other caught at the back of her neck, holding her powerless. His eyes were almost black now, glittering with emotion as they searched her face, and she was overwhelmingly aware of his naked body and the sheer animal strength of the muscles that rippled under the tanned skin.

'Back to your own room?' he rasped. 'And would you mind telling me just why? We were beginning to get somewhere at last—if it hadn't been for that damned phone call we'd have been in another world by now. So what's the problem? Still worried for your virginity, is that it? Well, I took pretty good care of that myself two years ago, but you don't expect me to believe it's lasted this long? Not with the way you were then, Libby? You were begging for it, you know you were—and I don't suppose that changed just because *I* wasn't on the scene any more!'

Libby stared at him helplessly. She knew that it would be almost impossible to persuade him that she had indeed remained a virgin since their engagement—that no other man had ever affected her the way Keir had, and still did. Even now, the warm virility emanating from his body was sending waves of desire surging through her, making her feel weak and dizzy. But she mustn't let them control her; however angry Keir's frustration might make him, this was one time when she *mustn't* give in.

'Well?' he growled. 'Are you going to give me an answer, or am I going to put an end to your blow-hot, blow-cold games by carrying you back to the bed and finishing what we started, by force if necessary?'

'*No!*' Libby panted, struggling frantically in his arms. 'No, Keir, you wouldn't—'

'Wouldn't I?' he taunted, pulling her closer. 'What makes you so sure of that, Libby?' Ignoring her gasp, he moved his body sensuously against hers, so that the rough towelling of the robe accentuated his hardness. 'Do you know something?' he growled, his breath warm in her ear. 'I'm beginning to wonder if this isn't all some game you're playing with me. It's all to do with that quarrel we had, isn't it? You're still holding some deep grudge against me and this is your way of punishing me—come out here and flaunt yourself at me, knowing I'm vulnerable, knowing I don't remember anything about it and can only remember being in love with you. My God!' He held her away from him and stared down at her, his face pale and a muscle twitching in his cheek. '*Is* that it, Libby? Is this some hellish kind of punishment you're inflicting on me? Because if it is, I swear I'll make you sorry for it! Your nasty little game has backfired badly, my sweet, and now *I'm* the one who's going to do the punishing!'

Libby's struggles became frantic, but they could have been the struggles of a butterfly for all the effect they had on Keir as he whipped her off her feet and carried her back to throw her on the bed. The gentleness he had displayed earlier had vanished as he flung himself down to cover her body, thrusting aside the robe with cruel fingers before he gripped both her wrists in one strong hand and pinned her flailing legs down with his own.

'Let me go!' Libby cried, using her teeth as her only weapon and biting the hard shoulder that was all she could reach. 'Keir, I beg you—don't do it! I wasn't trying to punish you, you've got it all wrong. Keir, you're *hurting* me—let me go, let me *go*!'

Keir raised his head slightly and his eyes met hers. She quailed at the expression in them; it was a look of almost maniacal fury, a look she had never encountered before. But even in her fear, she could understand what had brought that look there. All the bewilderment and frustrations of the past months, culminating in her own appearance and the difficulties of their own relationship, known only to her while Keir was, in his own mind, simply in love with her—all that had led to the events of this evening and, just when Keir must have thought that everything was coming right, Pia had rung and Libby had tried to escape him yet again. No wonder he had given rein at last to those animal passions that were so near the surface and so firmly repressed. Keir had shown iron control, she thought, from the days of their engagement to the reunion. But nobody could repress every emotion and not suffer for it. And Keir was suffering now. And so was she!

All the same, she had to stop him somehow. She had to prevent him from unleashing those frightening forces of his darker side. And not just for her own sake—for his, too. He would never be able to forgive himself, she knew, if he lost control so far as to take her by force. Keir just wasn't that kind of man.

Keir was gathering himself now for the final battle, and she had to act quickly. Still dizzy from the closeness of his body, still half-longing to submit, Libby tensed her body against his and, as he lifted himself above her, pushed hard. He wasn't ready and she managed to draw her knees up, thrusting hard against his chest, then twisting sideways on the bed. She was half off it by the time Keir recovered and reached for her, but although he dragged her back he had lost his advantage and Libby remained curled up against him, resisting his efforts to uncoil her.

'Don't try me too far, Libby,' he muttered between his teeth, and laid his mouth on hers.

His lips bruised hers but Libby let him part them; then she bit hard, past caring what injury she might inflict, and to her relief Keir jerked back, letting go of her so that she could twist right off the bed and grab the robe on her way to the door.

'You little fiend!' he ground out, but Libby had the door open before he could follow her this time and stood there, knowing she could slam it before he reached her.

'Don't come after me again, Keir,' she warned him. 'I'll fight you tooth and nail—and I mean that literally.' She bit her own lip, regretting her violence, but aware that it had been necessary, for Keir's self-respect as much as for her own. 'You must know it won't work that way,' she went on, half-pleadingly. 'You're not the kind of man to enjoy rape—and that's what it would have been. Keir, there's no future for us until we've got things straight—between us, and between you and Pia. It isn't as simple as you think. She's *coming* here. You've got to keep clear of any other entanglements until you know just what the situation is with her.'

Keir stared at her, and she saw with thankfulness the anger die out of his eyes, leaving them oddly vulnerable. She wanted to rush back across the room, take him in her arms and comfort him, but that would be asking for trouble. Instead, she stayed where she was, feeling more confident now that the danger was passing.

'Pia?' he repeated blankly. 'The woman who phoned

just now? But what does she have to do with it—with me, with us? What do *you* know about Pia?'

He really didn't remember, Libby thought, still amazed at the complete black-out of memory Keir had suffered, and pitying him all over again. Was it any wonder that his temper sometimes got the better of him? She took courage and stepped back into the room. He had to know now—whatever Jeremy and the doctors might say.

'Pia is an Italian lady,' she told him quietly. 'A *contessa*. You met her in Rome, and you lived with her there.'

Keir stared at her. His shock was plain on his face. He shook his head slowly, several times, and passed his hand across his forehead.

'And Italian *contessa*?' he repeated slowly. 'In Rome? And I *lived* with her? Who told you this?'

'Jeremy. He was with you—he stayed in the *palazzo*, too. But his room was in another part from yours—and hers.'

Keir shook his head again. 'It's like hearing you lived before, in another age,' he said. 'Libby, I remember nothing of any of this—can you believe that?'

'Oh yes,' she said quietly. 'I can believe that.' Nobody could act that bewilderment, nobody could lose colour and look so lost, so aghast. It was quite plain that Pia meant nothing to him; that he had lost all memory of her.

But that didn't mean that he wouldn't love her when he *did* remember, Libby reminded herself. And she could see that the realisation was dawning in Keir's mind, too, as his eyes searched hers.

'What else did Jeremy say?' he demanded urgently. 'He must have told you more than that. How far our—association—had progressed? Were we still—were we still together when I came to Malta? Why wasn't she with me then—or had we broken? You must tell me, Libby!'

'But I can't! Jeremy can't! He doesn't know—do you think I didn't ask him? He went back to London while you were still at the *palazzo*, and then came on to Malta. You never told him anything about Pia, and then you had your accident. He didn't know whether to contact her or not, and when he did try she had left Rome. There was nothing else he could do.'

'Oh God,' he said. 'And now she's coming here—soon, she said on the phone. And I won't even recognise her. Libby, I'm sorry—sorry about everything.' His eyes were pools of agony as he looked at her. 'You'd have been better to have stayed away from Malta. I've just dragged you into one hell of a mess and God knows what's going to happen next. But will you believe me that I *do*, as far as I can possibly tell, love you—in spite of my appalling behaviour just now.' He winced at the memory. 'I behaved like an animal. I'm sorry, Libby.'

Libby looked at him and her defences melted. Without giving herself time to think about the wisdom of her action, she walked quickly across the room and stood beside the bed. Keir looked up at her and she laid her hands on his cheeks.

'Don't worry about it, Keir,' she said softly, drawing his head to rest against her body. 'It's over now. Let's forget it.'

'I'm not likely to do that,' he muttered ruefully. 'I've never treated any woman that way before—and that it had to be *you* . . . No, I won't forget it.' He brought his hands up to hold hers against his face. 'Stay with me, Libby,' he muttered. 'I don't want to be alone tonight. Stay with me—I promise you nothing will happen.'

Libby's hesitation was no more than a second. She drew back the rumpled coverlet and lay down beside

Keir, still wrapped in the terry robe. Then she drew the coverlet over them both and turned towards Keir as naturally as if they had been sharing a bed for years. He slid his arms around her and she lay quietly against his body; and within minutes they were both fast asleep.

The sun was high in the sky when Libby stirred at last, and she realised that they had not closed the shutters the previous night. The warm shafts of light lay across the bed, turning the darkness of the burgundy silk to a deep pink. Libby lay quite still, looking round the unfamiliar room, as the memories of last night filled her mind.

Had she done right in staying with Keir? She was still clasped in his arms and the warmth of his body, so relaxed in sleep that it felt almost boneless, gave her a feeling of rightness. Keir was right—this was how they were meant to be. And would have been, but for Pia.

She turned her head slightly so that she could see his face. It looked younger now, more vulnerable with the defensive lines smoothed away and the reserve gone. The harshness, too, had disappeared from his chiselled lips and there was a tenderness in their curve that she recognised with a pang, realising that she had forgotten he could look just like that. Since his accident, she guessed, he had found it necessary to retreat behind his own barriers, and certainly that had been the case since her own arrival.

Libby shifted very slightly, wanting to see if she could get out of the bed without waking Keir. He stirred as she moved out of his arms, and she stiffened, afraid that he would wake; in spite of his promise, she wasn't at all sure what his reactions might be if he woke and found her in his arms, in his bed. They might be the normal reactions of any red-blooded male, and she didn't want to take the risk.

But Keir didn't wake; instead, he moved slightly away from Libby and she held her breath as he turned over, leaving her free to slip from her side of the bed and tiptoe quietly from the room. Outside, she leaned against the wall and took a deep breath of relief.

Right. Now she needed a shower and, after that, a lot of coffee. They might have got through the night safely, in the end, but there was a whole day to face now, and all the days to come. Which must inevitably include complications—Pia being the most important. Libby found that she didn't even know when the Italian *contessa* planned to arrive—had she told Keir? If she had, he hadn't mentioned it. But then, when Pia had spoken to him he hadn't realised the significance of her visit.

Thoughtfully, Libby showered and washed her hair, blowing it dry to a soft dark cap. Feeling somewhat better, she dressed in her coral pink outfit, and then went through to the tiny kitchen to make coffee.

Would it be better for her to leave now, go back to England? She'd already risked getting badly hurt by staying, and last night could have been even more traumatic than it had. She sighed impatiently; what was wrong with her? She *wanted* Keir to make love to her, didn't she? Yes, but not like that, she answered. That could have spoiled everything, made any future for them impossible.

But what future did they have anyway—with Pia on the doorstop?

By the time she took her coffee out to the balcony, Libby was no nearer an answer. She decided not to try to find one any more. Just wait and see which way the wind blew. A lot depended on Pia's attitude—was she still in love with Keir, for instance? It hadn't occurred to Libby before that she might not be. And did she know about Keir's accident? Presumably not, since Jeremy hadn't been able to contact her and there was no one else, as far as Libby knew, who might have done so. Keir had no family, she knew that; an only child of only children, his parents had both died some years earlier and he had been quite alone in the world. So it didn't seem likely that Pia could have found out about the accident from anyone else.

Perhaps her arrival on Malta had already been arranged—before Keir had even left Rome. But if they had still been together, wouldn't she have contacted him before this? Wouldn't she have written, phoned?

Libby was quite glad to have her thoughts interrupted when the door to the flat opened and Jeremy came in, breezy as usual, his shaggy beard almost bristling with energy and goodwill. He swung out to the balcony and was halfway through an exuberant greeting when he stopped dead and stared at Libby, a look of concern creasing his cheerful face.

'Libby? What the hell's the matter with you? You look like death warmed up.'

'Thanks,' she said dryly. 'That makes me feel a lot better! You're a real tonic, Jeremy, do you know that?'

'Sorry,' he said, sitting down and reaching for the coffee pot. 'Didn't mean to sound quite so unflattering, but you do look a bit washed out. What is it? And where's Keir?'

'Still in bed,' Libby told him, and then sighed as a look of amused comprehension spread over Jeremy's face. 'And you needn't look like that! It's not like that at all. At least—' She caught herself up as Jeremy's grin grew wider. 'Jeremy, it's not funny. Keir had a phone call last night. From Pia. She's coming here.'

'*Pia* is?' Jeremy whistled softly. 'Well, I guess that's enough to keep anyone awake at nights! What was his reaction?'

Libby shrugged. 'He didn't know who she was. Didn't seem to react at all. I had to tell him.'

'You did? Well, I suppose you hadn't much choice.' Jeremy frowned. 'And then what? Did he have any memory at all?'

'No. He said it was like being told about a previous incarnation. But well, you know how he is about me. He still thinks he's in love with me and this *contessa* isn't going to make any difference.' Libby raised troubled grey eyes to Jeremy's face. 'But she is, isn't she? Keir must have loved her, too. How is he going to feel when he sees her again? It might all come back—and then he'll hate me all over again.' Her voice shook. 'And I don't think I can bear to be here when that happens, Jeremy.'

'No, I can see that.' Jeremy sucked in his lips. 'Not an easy situation for anyone, is it? Even Pia—coming here expecting God knows what. If only we knew what the situation was between them before Keir left Rome. But Pia's the only one who knows that, and she's the one person we can't ask.' He shook his head. 'Did she say when she'll be arriving?'

'I'm not sure. Keir didn't say.'

'Well, I guess—' Jeremy broke off as they heard sounds from inside the flat, and they both turned to see Keir coming through the big glass door, dressed in his towelling robe and rubbing his tousled hair.

'Oh, there you are, Libby,' he said. 'I've been looking for you everywhere. I woke up and you were gone—why didn't—' He caught sight of Jeremy and stopped, and Libby felt her face flame as she saw Jeremy's mouth twitch again. Well, there wasn't much use in denying what he obviously—and quite naturally—thought. She got up and went past Keir to fetch another mug. Perhaps Keir could do some explaining for a change.

She didn't know, when she came back, whether he

had done so or not. The two men were sitting at the table talking in low voices, and when she walked through the door they broke off quickly and turned towards her almost guiltily.

'Jeremy's been telling me about Pia,' Keir said, and there was an odd note, almost an apology, in his voice. 'It's more or less as you said, Libby—not much more to it. So we're no further forward, I'm afraid.

'And you don't know when she's coming?' Libby asked, pouring coffee.

Keir shrugged. 'No idea. She simply said—as far as I remember, I wasn't paying too much attention at the time—that she was coming and would be with me soon.' He glanced at Jeremy with something like desperation. 'I suppose I'll have to meet her, but I don't even know what she looks like. You'll have to come with me, Jeremy. At least you know her.'

'Can't see that exactly being welcomed,' Jeremy remarked, 'but I suppose you're right. You know, this whole thing is getting crazier and crazier. I never realised a lost memory could cause so much trouble.'

'Well, at least it can't cause much more than this,' Keir said gloomily, drinking his coffee and staring out to sea.

Libby looked at him. He was looking tired now, and older than he had when she had watched him sleeping. She hoped he was right in saying that there couldn't be much more trouble to come—but she had an uneasy feeling that he might be wrong.

'Look,' she said, making up her mind, 'wouldn't it be better if I made myself scarce? It's going to be bad enough for you, Keir, meeting this *contessa*, without me being on the scene. I think I'd better go—into Valletta, perhaps, or even back to England. I—'

'Go?' Keir raised his head and stared at her. 'Go? Libby, you can't mean it. When I need you more than ever before? You can't run out on me now.'

'But how do I *know* you need me?' Libby asked. Out of the corner of her eye she was aware of Jeremy, getting up quietly and leaving them together, and was grateful for his diplomacy. 'You may not need me at all—you may see Pia and remember everything, including the fact that you hate me.' She couldn't help her voice trembling as she said that; now, more than ever, she knew how badly she needed Keir to love her, not hate her. 'Keir, it can only make things worse if I'm here. Let me go, at least until you know where you are—'

'I know where I am now,' he broke in. 'With the girl I love. And that isn't any Italian *contessa*, it's you. Haven't you got that into that stubborn little head of yours yet? Just what do I have to do to prove it to you?'

'You don't have to do anything,' Libby told him through a shine of tears. 'I believe you, Keir, but I can't forget that your mind is still back on Dartmoor, two years ago. I believed you then, too—and then it all changed. *It could change again*, don't you see? And you've loved Pia since that time. How can I be sure, how can *you* be sure, that you won't love her again?'

'Because I never *did* love her!' Keir exclaimed in exasperation. 'Libby, I *couldn't* have loved her—I've loved *you* all the time. Whatever there was between me and Pia, it was never real, not like you and I had between us. God, I'd lost you, hadn't I—I hadn't seen you for what, a year, eighteen months—I didn't expect ever to see you again. Do you expect me to have lived like a monk all that time? For the rest of my life? But that didn't mean I was going to *love* any other woman. It was something completely separate.'

Libby gazed at him. It could all be true. But there was no way she could be sure—until Pia herself had arrived and made the situation clear.

'I still think I ought to go,' she said stubbornly. 'All right, I won't leave Malta, but I can't stay in this flat. What is she going to think if she finds me here?'

'She won't think anything,' Keir said flatly, 'because I shall tell her. I shall tell her about you and what—'

'Keir, you *can't*!' Libby was beginning to feel almost sorry for the *contessa*, arriving to so many shocks. She tried to imagine herself in the other girl's place. 'Look, whatever you feel about her, she may genuinely love *you*. Haven't you thought of that? Don't be too cruel, Keir.'

I must be mad, she thought miserably. *I* love Keir, and he says he loves me, yet here I am doing all I can to push him into another woman's arms. I'm crazy, I just have to be.

Well, there was a limit to how altruistic anyone could be, and she certainly wasn't going to try much harder. But, almost to her disappointment, Keir didn't push her any further. He stared out down the valley towards the sea where the gaily-painted little boats were carrying more loads of tourists to see the beauties of the Blue Grotto, and said no more. He seemed almost to forget that Libby was there, and after a few moments she got up and went quietly back into the flat.

Jeremy was in the kitchen, making a sandwich from a fresh Maltese loaf he must have brought with him, and some ham. He turned enquiringly as Libby came in, and she sat down wearily at the table.

'He insists she means nothing to him,' she reported. 'But we can't be sure of that, can we? Jeremy, I just don't know how to cope. He won't let me go back to England, doesn't even want me to move out of the flat. It's going to be an impossible situation for all of us. I just don't know what to do!'

Jeremy eyed her thoughtfully. 'What do you *want* to

do? I mean, what would you do if there were no complications?'

'If Keir hadn't lost his memory, you mean?' Libby shrugged. 'Well, if he wanted me I'd marry him. But then, he probably wouldn't want me—in fact, I'm sure he wouldn't or he'd have come for me before.'

'Unless he was equally sure *you* wouldn't want *him*. All right, let's suppose that he did remember everything, and still wanted you. What would you do then?'

'Whatever he wanted,' Libby said simply. 'It was my fault, you know, that we broke up. I—I blamed Keir for something that happened—my father dying. I was upset and overwrought, and my mother was so bitter, that I sent him away. It was all totally unfair and Keir was quite justified in never wanting to see me again. And he's going to feel like that again, when he remembers. That's why I wanted to tell him the truth—and now, I wish I had!' She covered her face with her hands, feeling the hopelessness of the situation like a deep, dark well into which she was being dragged.

Jeremy was silent. He finished making his sandwich, but he didn't eat it. Instead, he stood looking down into the road, watching the Maltese women who stood in chattering groups on the corner. The sound of their voices rose into the kitchen, a cheerful hubbub that seemed worlds away from the despair that Libby was feeling.

'I really think I'd better go,' she said in a low voice. 'I just don't want to be here when Pia arrives, Jeremy. I don't want to see the look on Keir's face when they meet.'

'I'm sorry, Libby,' Jeremy said, his voice oddly quiet. 'I think you've left it too late. There's a car drawing up outside—and if I'm not very much mistaken, that's Pia herself, getting out of it.' He turned and faced Libby, his brown eyes grave. 'Try not to worry, Libby, I'll be here if you need anyone to turn to. But you're going to have to face it.' He put both hands on her shoulders and gave her a quick, firm kiss. 'All I can say now is—good luck!'

He went swiftly through the flat to warn Keir, and Libby stared after him before going to the window herself to look down. The woman below was just paying off a taxi, and Libby could see little more than the top of her head. And then she turned and glanced around her, looking up at the flats, and Libby gasped and drew back.

Good luck! She was going to need more than luck if she hoped to keep Keir's love in the face of this girl's opposition. She was just about the most beautiful woman Libby had ever seen. And she didn't look likely to be thwarted by a dark-haired little English girl. The Italian *contessa* looked the kind of woman who got what she wanted—every time.

CHAPTER SEVEN

PIA had evidently known just which of the flats was Keir's, and she was at the door before any of them could go down to meet her. Libby, still frozen in the kitchen, heard the bell chime and then footsteps going through the hall. The door opened and there was a murmur of voices, and she closed her eyes, wondering just how Keir was feeling as he saw the woman he had lived with and now did not remember.

'Libby,' said a soft voice, and her eyes flew open. She stared dazedly at Keir, who hadn't gone to the door after all, but was standing close to her in the kitchen. It must have been Jeremy who had gone to let Pia in . . . Her eyes were wide, almost silver as she looked up at Keir. Oh, if only she'd left days ago! This was a situation she just couldn't cope with.

'Go on, Keir,' she said, trying to keep her voice steady. 'You've got a visitor. Don't skulk out in the kitchen and keep her waiting.'

He glanced down expressively at the towelling robe that was his only covering, and Libby added with a bitterness that surprised them both: 'You needn't worry. I'm sure she's seen you like that plenty of times!'

She saw his lips tighten at that, and felt sorry at once. It wasn't Keir's fault that this situation had arisen. But before she could speak, he turned away and she knew by the set of his back that she had touched a raw nerve. And then the murmur of voices became louder, and Jeremy appeared in the doorway.

'Pia's here, Keir,' he said quietly. 'She's out on the balcony. Will you come?'

Keir shook his head decisively. 'Not until I've showered and dressed,' he said, and Libby realised that he was nervous of this strange reunion. 'Give her some coffee, Jeremy, will you, and—and talk to her.' He glanced uncertainly at Libby and she waited for him to suggest that she too went out to keep his mistress—*ex*-mistress?—company. But he didn't, he just shrugged helplessly and once again she felt sorry for the position he was in.

'I'll go out,' she said quickly. 'No, Jeremy, I can only be an embarrassment. I'll catch the bus into Valletta and do some shopping. I've been wanting the chance to have another look around there.'

But none of them was allowed to carry out these plans, for at that moment a shadow fell across the doorway and a husky voice broke in on their words. Pia had evidently grown tired of waiting—and had come to look for Keir herself.

'So this is where you hide yourself, *caro*!' she said, and the three of them looked round, startled and confused. Pia, however, was completely in command. Tall, with a voluptuous figure that narrowed in to a tiny waist, she surveyed them through deep violet eyes under a mass of rich, bronze hair that fell in shining waves past her bare shoulders. A smile hovered round her full lips and Libby saw small white teeth catch provocatively at the lower lip before she spoke again. 'Keir, why are you *lurking* in a corner like this? Aren't you pleased to see me?'

Keir moved slowly forward. He was looking at her and Libby felt a stab of fear. Had he already remembered? Did he recognise Pia as the woman whose *palazzo* he had shared—as the woman he loved? But his sapphire eyes, although intent, gave away nothing.

Pia seemed to have no inhibitions, but perhaps Jeremy hadn't had time to explain the situation. She moved forward to meet Keir, her body graceful and sensuous as she raised her arms to link them behind his head and pressed her curves lightly against his body. She was almost as tall as he was, and her lips touched his with only a slight raising of her body on her toes. For what seemed an age, they stood together, lips meeting, and Libby turned away, unable to watch. Then Pia dropped lightly back and her voice was cool as she said: '*Not* pleased to see me after all, *caro*? That was not the kiss I expected after so many weeks apart. Or perhaps—' she flicked a glance over Jeremy and Libby '—perhaps you prefer more privacy for our first meeting. Send them away—Jeremy and your maid.'

'*Maid?*' Keir exclaimed, and Libby felt the colour flood into her face. Surely he wasn't going to tell Pia the whole story now—here in the crowded little kitchen. He evidently realised what she was thinking and his lips twitched. 'All right, Pia. Let's go back to the balcony and you can tell me about your journey. Where have you come from, what have you been doing?' He was searching for clues, Libby realised, and thought how difficult this must be for him. *Hadn't* Jeremy told Pia anything?

Pia's delicate brows crinkled with doubt as she looked at Keir. She put out a hand and drew her fingertips slowly down the towelling sleeve of his robe, then slid them up inside over his skin. Libby saw him shiver slightly. He would never be able to resist this woman, she thought desolately. Even if he didn't remember her, the *contessa* would win him all over again with ease; she knew all the tricks, and Libby had to admit that as a couple they were perfectly matched.

'Poor Keir,' Pia said softly in her throaty voice. 'Jeremy told me that you had had an accident and couldn't always remember things. But you will be all right now, *caro mio*. I will help you to remember. How could you forget the happiness we shared? It will all come back, I promise you.'

Her hand still on his wrist inside the loose sleeve, she drew him through the door; and as she turned, she gave Libby a flashing glance. 'Make some fresh coffee, will you?' she commanded. 'And bring out some orange juice, freshly squeezed, and something to eat. I have been travelling and I am hungry.'

Libby took a breath, but Keir gave her a warning glance and she subsided. He had promised to tell Pia the truth, and she could only hope that he would. She forgot that she had been on the verge of feeling sorry for the unknown *contessa*. That had been before she saw her. Now, she knew that Pia needed nobody else to fight her battles. She could look after herself—no matter who else got hurt in the process.

'Well?' Jeremy murmured in her ear. 'What are you waiting for? Coffee, the lady ordered. And orange juice. And "something to eat". Aren't you going to get on with it?'

Libby looked at him witheringly. 'No, I'm not,' she said in a terse voice. 'That woman's just trying to put me down. She knows full well I'm not a maid, she's just asserting her own superiority. She can make her own coffee and squeeze her own oranges—I'm not waiting on her!'

Jeremy grinned. 'Well said,' he approved. 'I see you have the same view of the beautiful *contessa* as I have. *I* won't make her any coffee, either. Although, as Keir's employee, I suppose she has more right to expect me to do it.'

Libby wandered over to the window and stared down. The taxi had gone, and so had the chattering women.

The street was deserted, hot and empty in the late morning sun. She wondered what would happen next, and what she ought to do. She could go back to the balcony, of course—but she just couldn't face Pia again, and her blatant attempts to attract Keir.

Well, she wouldn't have to try for very long, Libby thought. She was clearly experienced with men, and with Keir in particular. She would know just what had attracted him before, and a repeat performance would be no trouble at all.

She went back to her own room and stood there, undecided. Through the open window came the murmur of voices—Keir and Pia, on the balcony. Tension gripped her body like a cramp, and she sat down on the bed, hands clasped together. The whole situation was impossible! How could she stay here now? Pia had brought suitcases, though Libby doubted whether the *contessa* had carried them to the flat herself. But she evidently meant to stay and although there was another bedroom, Libby didn't think Pia would expect to use it. No, there just wasn't room for three of them, and Libby didn't have much hope that her being on the spot first would give her precedence—in Pia's eyes, at least.

She got up and moved over to the window. Why *shouldn't* it, she thought suddenly. Why shouldn't her presence here be as important as Pia's arrival? *She* was the one Keir remembered and believed himself to be in love with; she was the one he wanted, at the moment anyway. You've got all the cards in your hand, she told herself sternly. Surely you're not going to throw them down on the table and leave the game! Get out there and fight!

A new determination flooded her with energy, and she took a quick look in the mirror. All right, she couldn't cope with Pia's voluptuous beauty, but she wasn't bad-looking in her own gamin way. She flicked a brush through her short black hair and added a fresh touch of pink lipstick to match her dress. Then she took a deep breath and went out through the flat to the balcony.

Pia was lying in the sun-lounger beside Keir. She was wearing a pants suits of cream silk and she had discarded the jacket to reveal a low-cut top in emerald green that clung like a second skin to her full breasts. The bronze hair fell in shining waves across her neck and as Libby appeared she lifted red-tipped fingers to push it away from the slender column.

She glanced up at Libby and her delicate brows came together in a frown of annoyance.

'You have been a long time with the coffee,' she complained. 'And where is it? Don't tell me you forgot.'

'No, I didn't forget.' Libby looked back steadily, then took one of the sun-chairs. 'I didn't make any. We'd had our breakfast.'

'You didn't make any?' Pia's eyes flashed dangerously. 'Keir, is this the way you greet your guests?'

'Not normally,' he answered pleasantly, 'but then Libby is my guest too. Not a maid, as you took her to be.' He had taken the opportunity to dress quickly in dark blue shorts and shirt, Libby noticed, and even at that moment couldn't help her eyes lingering on the fine hairs that covered his well-muscled thighs. But she could learn nothing from his face; he seemed to have withdrawn into his own private world and watched the two girls with enigmatic eyes.

'Your guest?' Pia looked disconcerted. 'A relative, perhaps?' She smiled charmingly at Libby. 'Forgive me, but how was I to know? Keir has never mentioned any female relatives to me.'

'No, I'm not a relative. Just—just an old friend.' Libby felt herself colour as she answered. What else could she say? She wasn't Keir's fiancée any more—she couldn't even describe herself as his girl-friend. 'I—heard about his accident and came out to see if I could do anything,' she hurried on. That was more or less the truth, anyway.

'Oh yes, the accident. Keir, you still have not told me about that. What happened to you, *caro*? And can you really not remember?'

Keir shrugged. 'I don't know what happened, Pia. Apparently I was water-skiing and something went wrong. I gave my head a bang and woke up in hospital, but I don't remember anything of it. I just have to believe what other people tell me.'

'But that is terrible.' Pia gazed at him with wide amethyst eyes. 'To forget, so. The accident—well, it is no bad thing to forget *that*. But the other things—how much is it you have forgotten, *caro mio*? Tell me what you remember.'

'Nothing of the past two years,' Keir told her, and the violet eyes widened with shock. 'The last memory I have is of being in England—with Libby.' His voice had been harsh, but it softened as he added: 'I'm afraid I don't remember you at all, Pia. As far as I'm concerned, I've met you for the first time this morning.'

There was a long silence. Pia stared at Keir's face, her eyes searching as if trying to drill through to the truth. Her face was pale and Libby felt a flash of unexpected sympathy. But it vanished when she saw the vicious glance that the other girl flicked at her before she spoke.

'And you?' she asked softly, but with an unpleasant edge to her tone. 'Are you too forgotten, after that last memory? Is that why you are here, to persuade Keir that all was well between you?'

'No, it's not—I had no idea—' Libby stopped abruptly. Did Pia *know* about her and Keir? Had he confided in her, told her about their quarrel? Her face burned at the thought and she turned away quickly.

'You had no idea?' Pia pursued relentlessly. 'No idea of what? Of his accident? Of his amnesia? So why did you come, tell me that, flying to his side when you had not been near him for so long? Just what did you hope to gain?'

Keir intervened, his voice cold. 'Libby came because I wrote and asked her to come.' He didn't add that he had subsequently forgotten doing so, and Libby threw him a grateful glance. But Pia was even less pleased by his answer.

She did not show it to Keir, however. Giving Libby a glance of dislike that he couldn't see, she leaned over and laid her fingertips on Keir's bare arm.

'It will be all right, *caro*,' she murmured softly. 'Everything will be all right now. I will help you to remember—you cannot forget what we had together, nobody could. And this little English miss can go home, there will be nothing for her to do here.'

Keir lay very still. His eyes were shadowed and there was no way of guessing what his reaction was to Pia's caressing fingertips. But he had succumbed to her charm once—was there any reason why he shouldn't do so again?

Libby looked up with relief as Jeremy came out on to the balcony, carrying a tray. The welcome scent of coffee floated through the air, and Libby smiled at him gratefully as he set the tray on the table and took the chair beside her. He poured out four mugs and handed them round.

'At least someone has some manners,' Pia said pointedly as she accepted hers with another charming smile at Jeremy. 'It's good to see you again, Jeremy. Tell me about your trip to London, did it go well? And here on Malta—are you staying here in the flat?'

'No, I've got a room at the other end of the village. I'd got settled in there before I organised this place, and they treat me pretty well so I decided to stay.'

'Ah.' A gleam of satisfaction showed in Pia's luminous eyes. 'So there will be plenty of room for me to stay, hm? And you—' she turned to Libby. '—when do you go back to England?'

'I haven't decided yet,' Libby said shortly. 'And I *am* staying in the flat.' She caught Keir's sardonic eye and blushed. 'As long as Keir wants me, that is.'

'Oh, but surely it is clear that he will *not* want you!' Pia moved a little closer to Keir and slid her hand down his arm so that their fingers interlocked. '*I* am here now, and I can help him so much. I have been with him for quite a long time, you see, and I know all his recent life. Whereas you—' she shrugged, dismissing Libby's time with Keir as of no importance. 'I think it will be best if you go back quite soon,' she finished simply.

Libby looked at her, lying there on the sun-lounger, close to Keir, her arm linked with his. A sudden cold fear touched her heart. Was the Italian girl right? She was, after all, only saying what Libby herself had said earlier. She knew more about Keir than Libby could hope to. And what was the point in fighting when Keir himself might remember at any time?

'Keir?' she said uncertainly. It was almost impossible to judge his reactions now. He had told Pia she was still a stranger to him. He had been reluctant to meet her, insisted that Libby still held his heart. Yet now—there he was, letting Pia touch him and caress him, looking for all the world as if he was *enjoying* it. As he probably was, Libby thought bitterly. What man wouldn't? Pia was a very attractive woman.

Keir turned his head and looked at Libby, but his eyes

were still veiled and she had no idea what he might be thinking. She felt helpless and angry. Why didn't he *say* something—give her some hint? But the silence stretched between them, and Pia made a tiny sound of triumph and lay back on her lounger, one arm raised above her head to accentuate the flowing lines of her body.

Suddenly, Libby could stand it no longer. She jumped to her feet and ran back into the flat. Footsteps followed her, but she didn't pause to see who it was; she grabbed her bag and a cotton jacket and jerked open the door, slamming it behind her as she ignored the lift and stumbled down the stairs.

So she might be acting irrationally, she thought as she came out into the blinding sunlight. Who wouldn't, when they had just been through a night and a morning such as she had just experienced? All she knew was that she had to get away—alone somewhere—where she could sort out her confused thoughts and decide just what it would be best to do next.

Best for whom, she wondered dully as she reached the main square of the village and found a bus just about to leave. For Keir? Or for herself?

One thing she did know—she wasn't wasting any more feeling on Pia. That lady didn't need anyone's compassion. And she wouldn't have any trouble deciding what to do for the best, either. Pia knew very well what she wanted, and she had already made up her mind to get it.

The bus rattled along the narrow roads, the noise of its engine almost drowned by the chattering of its passengers. Libby sat, hemmed in by a stout Maltese woman, gazing out of the window. She had had no idea where the bus was going and simply handed her money over to the driver as she boarded, nodding vaguely to his question and accepting her change without interest. Presumably he had taken a fare for the furthest point, and she would get off when everyone else did.

Not that it mattered. She was already beginning to regret her hasty flight from the flat—yet what else could she have done? Pia had shown all too clearly that she meant to oust Libby, and she was probably quite right in thinking she could. After all, Keir had lived with her, quite recently. It had probably been accepted between them that Pia should join him in Malta, and there really wasn't any reason why she should give way to a girl from Keir's past who had no claim whatsoever.

The more she thought about it, the more hopeless her own position seemed to be. I wish I'd never come, Libby thought miserably as she stared out at the brown, terraced fields and the white farmhouses with their flat roofs spread with drying gourds. I wouldn't have realised then that I still love Keir—I could have gone on in my own way, making a new life, perhaps even getting married . . . None of that seemed possible now. Her safe, settled life had been turned upside down and no other man would ever be able to satisfy her.

The bus was climbing now. Libby looked around at the other occupants, mostly Maltese; dark-haired, with sallow brown skin and sloe eyes. The older women were all rather plump, but there were a few younger girls with slim figures and attractive hairstyles. One or two of them had babies with them, bright-eyed and alert, and Libby smiled at one who was standing precariously on his mother's lap just in front, gazing back at her with unwinking eyes.

She wondered if the bus driver had as much confidence as he should in his own driving—his cubicle had been decorated as a shrine, festooned with holy pictures and little statues. She had noticed this in several vehicles—lorries, cars, buses, even motor-cycles all had their images of the Virgin Mary and other saints perched on ledges or dangling from the roof. Just as many of them—like the lorry she had seen when Jeremy had taken her to the Blue Grotto—had religious names. Though there were others that were rather more secular; she had seen one only yesterday with the name Johnny Cash emblazoned on its side!

The bus rumbled on, passing through several villages, and then stopped in Mosta. Most of the passengers got out here and Libby hesitated. The driver was still in his seat and hadn't stopped the engine, so she assumed that he was going on further. She wondered whether to get out anyway, but Mosta, bustling and noisy with traffic, didn't attract her in spite of the cathedral with its great dome that dominated the centre of the town, and she stayed in her seat.

A few more people boarded the bus and it jerked into life, blustering through the streaming traffic to get out of the town. Libby looked out of the window, trying to force herself to take an interest; she hadn't been to this part of the island before, but the stark scenery passed before her eyes like a dull travel film and her mind went back again to the flat in Zurrieq. It wouldn't matter where she was, she thought sadly; she could be looking at Niagara Falls and they would seem no more interesting. She just wasn't in the mood for sightseeing—she'd got on the bus as a means of escape, nothing more.

What was happening, back there in Zurrieq? One thing was sure, Pia would be taking every advantage of her absence. And Keir, from the way he had behaved, would be letting her. Why shouldn't he? He knew Pia and loved her, even if he had forgotten it—and Libby knew all too well how frustration had been building up in him during the past few days. Was he going to pass up the opportunity of relieving that frustration with a woman who was plainly only too ready to co-operate? And who would, afterwards, be in triumphant and final possession of her prize?

But Keir *wasn't* a prize, to be handed out on points. He had been unnaturally silent that morning, but that had been understandable. Once he had sorted things out in his own mind, the two women would have no choice but to accept his decision. But what would it be?

Libby shivered and wrenched her mind away from the problem. Nothing she could do now would make any difference—she had probably lost any chance she might have by running away. It was better to think about something else—let her mind and emotions rest for a few hours. She might then return refreshed and more able to cope with whatever came next.

The bus had climbed another hill and was now rumbling down towards the sea. Libby craned her neck, unable to escape a feeling of delight at the view—the prettiest she had so far seen on this rather austere island. Below them, and behind, lay St Paul's Bay, a cluster of buildings testifying to its popularity as a tourist centre. They had just run along the shore of the bay, looping around the blue waters, and people in bathing costumes had looked up from the sandy beach as they passed—the typical holiday scene, and for a moment Libby had wished she could join them. But she hadn't brought her bikini and in any case swimming and sunbathing weren't much fun alone. She had been glad when the bus began to ascend the hill out of the bay.

Now it was running down the other side and as St Paul's Bay disappeared a view of Mellieha Bay unfolded in front of them. Below stretched a valley more fertile than any Libby had seen so far, filled with lush vegetation; on the ridge stood the town of Mellieha and the sea twinkled beyond it like a bolt of shot silk, blue and glittering.

Well, if the bus went any further than this it could go without her, Libby decided. This was where she could roam in peace, enjoying the quiet, able to think. Later, she would have to return to the flat—but by then, with any luck, she would be more in command of herself, more able to cope with Pia's hostility. And with Keir—whatever mood he would be in by then.

This might well turn out to be her last day on Malta, she thought sadly. It would be a pity to leave without enjoying at least some of it.

Mellieha turned out to be just what Libby needed—a colourful but uncrowded little town, its main street corkscrewing down the hill. There were several interesting shops, and she stood entranced at the door of a bakery, watching the men take fresh loaves from the old ovens that went back like miniature caves into the thick rocky walls, replacing them with puffs of dough from the women working at the side.

Libby bought a loaf, unable to resist the appetising smell, and found some cheese to go with it. She wandered on around the town, explored the parish church, which seemed to be relatively new, and then discovered the original parish church, the Sanctuary of Our Lady. This was much more interesting; inside was an even older church, hewn from rock like a cave and decorated with murals. Libby looked at them, wondering just how old they were. That one of the Virgin and Child—was it the one Keir had told her was attributed to St Luke, who was supposed to have painted it when he was shipwrecked with St Paul? The attribution was wrong, Keir had said, but the mural was nevertheless very old. How far back this island's history went! She felt a pang that she would not be able to stay and see Keir's researches through. The character of Malta had caught at her imagination just as it had his, and she badly wanted to stay with him, a partner in his work, a partner in his whole life.

Oh Keir, Keir, she thought miserably if only we could turn the clock back. Back to that day on Dartmoor when we were so happy. If only I hadn't turned against you, if only I hadn't been so unfair, letting my mother's bitterness influence me against you. We could have been married by now, here together. And there would have been no lost years; no Pia.

She wandered into the tiny vestry and looked at the paintings and the offerings made by the many people who had made pilgrimages to the little church. Had their wishes been granted, she wondered. She hoped so. There was certainly an atmosphere of great peace in this ancient place.

Outside, the sun was dazzling. Libby looked around for somewhere to sit and eat her lunch, and caught her breath in astonishment.

Jeremy, his brown beard almost gold in the sunlight, his eyes twinkling with good humour and comfort, was sitting on a low wall as if waiting for her. And by the way he got up and came over, without the slightest surprise in his expression, that was just what he had been doing.

'Jeremy?' Libby said on a questioning note. 'Whatever are you doing here?'

'Looking for you, of course.' His voice was brisk and he smiled down at her. 'Hope you don't mind, Libby—I'll go away if you'd rather be on your own. But I was a bit worried when you dashed out like that, and I saw which bus you'd caught, so I thought I'd mooch around for a bit to see if I could find you. Saw you going into the sanctuary and waited till you came out. Just say if you'd rather I went,' he added quietly.

'No—no, I don't want you to go.' Libby looked up at him and felt suddenly what a very nice man he was, what was called a tower of strength. You could rest against that broad body and know that no harm would come to you, she thought, and wished that it could be Jeremy she had fallen in love with. But things were never that simple. She smiled at him and saw the relief in his eyes. He'd been really worried, she realised, and felt a warmth that somebody on this island cared about her.

'I've got some fresh bread,' she said, 'and some cheese. Too much for me to eat. Will you share it?'

'Thought you'd never ask!' Jeremy grinned. 'And I've got a bottle of wine in my car, so what more could we want? Let's drive down to the shore, shall we?'

They walked back to Jeremy's car and drove down the hill, past Mellieha Bay where little knots of people were sunbathing and swimming, and found a quiet spot near the Gozo ferry, where they could take their food down to the rocks and sit hidden from the road, watching the waves foam on the shore.

'What—what was happening at the flat?' Libby asked at last, breaking off a piece of delicious bread. 'Do you think Keir does remember Pia?'

Jeremy shrugged. 'Difficult to tell, he can play his cards very close to his chest when he likes, but I don't think so. I think he was keeping a low profile, trying to assess her, see whether he felt the same, or felt anything at all.' Jeremy glanced at Libby with serious brown eyes. 'I don't think anyone can really know just what it's like to lose part of one's life, the way Keir has. And especially with the complications there are in his case.'

'You mean, remembering me?' Libby looked rueful. 'Jeremy, I almost wish he'd forgotten me too! Then he would never have written, asking me to come. It couldn't have been any worse than it is now. He might have accepted Pia, even if he didn't remember her—' her voice broke at the thought but she kept on '—and I would have gone on with my own life, not knowing anything about it.'

'And would you rather it had been that way?' Jeremy asked quietly. 'You aren't fooling yourself, Libby. You know how you feel about Keir. At least this way you've got a chance—a fighting chance. Would you really rather not have had that?'

Libby sighed. 'Oh, I don't know. I honestly don't know. Well—yes, I suppose you're right. But I've blown it, haven't I? I've had my chance and I didn't take it. And now Pia's here and she's not going to miss any chances. I might as well pack up and go home.'

'And then you won't have any chance at all,' Jeremy warned her. 'Don't give up now, Libby. Not if you really want Keir. Stay by him—as long as you're here, there's hope.'

A tiny sparkle of laughter glittered in Libby's sea-grey eyes as she glanced up. 'Am I to take it you're on my side, Jeremy?' she asked, and his beard jutted as he answered:

'Yours and Keir's. Pia's an attractive woman, I'm not denying that. But she isn't right for Keir. I always knew that, though there was damned little I could do about it, and anyway I thought it would all fizzle out, burn itself up. And I never really knew what sort of girl *would* be right for him—until you arrived.' He put his hand over Libby's and she was surprised by the intensity of his voice as he went on. 'Don't run out on him now, Libby. He needs you, like he's never needed anyone before. Oh, I know how you feel—you're afraid that he'll remember that old quarrel and hate you again. But I don't reckon he ever did hate you. I think he understood just what happened—and he was waiting till the time came to get together again. Pia and the others were just ways of passing the time. And when he remembers—he'll remember that.'

Libby sighed again. If only she could believe it. She wanted to, oh so badly. And why not? a little voice argued. Jeremy could so easily be right. He knew Keir probably better than anyone. He had worked with him, accompanied him all over the world. Wouldn't he know about this?

But he could also be wrong—disastrously wrong. And Libby couldn't let herself take the risk of believing in something that might shatter under her touch like spun glass under a hammer.

'So what do I do?' she asked, speaking as much to herself as to Jeremy. 'Go back to the flat? I don't even know if Pia's staying there, but it certainly looked as if she meant to. And if she is—it'll be impossible, Jeremy, can't you see that?'

'So you mean to let her push you out? Like a cuckoo pushing out the rightful occupants of the nest? Libby, you'll lose everything if you do that. Pia's a fighter, don't you realise, and she won't fight by the rules. She wants Keir, and she wants him badly. But she doesn't *love* him—not the way you do.' Jeremy paused, then went on quietly: 'you *do* love Keir, Libby, are you going to condemn him to *that*? A loveless marriage with a predatory woman? Forget about yourself—think about *him*.'

His words struck home and Libby caught her breath. Of course, he was right! She couldn't just step back and let Pia take over. In ordinary circumstances, yes—Keir was a grown man, adult enough to make his own decisions, right or wrong. But as things were—Pia was out to take advantage of him. Only the Italian girl knew the truth of the relationship between her and Keir and she wouldn't scruple to use her knowledge—or hide it—to get what she wanted. Jeremy had thought it was just an affair, more serious than some of the others, but still likely to burn itself out. And he could be right. So how could Libby leave, knowing that Keir, who knew no better, could easily be persuaded otherwise by the Italian *contessa* who had made up her mind to marry him.

She took a deep breath and faced Jeremy. Her face was pale but set, her brows a delicate black line across her smooth brow, her lips firm.

'All right,' she said. 'I'll go back. And I'll stay—if Keir wants me. And as long as he wants me.'

'That's my girl,' Jeremy said approvingly. 'And now, if you don't mind, I'd like a little siesta here in the sun. And then we'll make our way back at a leisurely pace to Zurrieq, all right? Don't worry, Libby, if anything was going to happen between those two, it would have happened by now. But I have a feeling Pia's in for a surprise or two. She's going to find Keir a rather harder nut to crack than she did in Rome—and I think the experience is going to be good for her!'

The flat was quiet when Libby finally returned, with only a few low lights to indicate that it was occupied at all. She hesitated at the door, reluctant to go in; but there was no sound from any of the rooms and she entered cautiously.

Where were Keir and Pia, she wondered. Late as it was, it wasn't difficult to imagine and she turned her mind away quickly from the thought of them sharing that big bed with its deep burgundy coverlet where she had lain with Keir—could it really be only last night? She wished for a moment that she had come back earlier, not allowed Jeremy to keep her out having a meal in Mellieha, with that long drive home afterwards, but she knew that he had been right really. An earlier return could only have been embarrassing for everyone, and she had to sort out her own feelings before exposing them once again to Pia's mocking gaze.

'What will you do, then?' Jeremy had asked as they sat eating their meal in The Arches restaurant. 'Just sit tight? Or are you going to fight Pia with her own weapons?'

'Arrogance and seductiveness?' Libby said wryly. 'I don't think they're quite me, Jeremy. No—I'll just have to be myself. After all, that's what Keir has to choose—if he chooses at all. I wouldn't blame him if he got tired of the whole thing and sent us both packing! But it isn't any use my trying to be what I'm not. That just makes more trouble.'

'Mm, I think you're right.' Jeremy's bright brown eyes regarded her with speculation. 'And a very nice self it is, too. I wonder . . .'

'Wonder what?' Libby forked up some *cannelloni*. She had little appetite, in spite of her long day out, but the food was very good and she had to eat it for Jeremy's sake.

Jeremy looked embarrassed. 'Nothing. Well, I was just wandering . . . Libby, if all this *doesn't* work out, if you do find yourself going back to London—well, you know I'll always be around, don't you?'

Libby looked up at him, startled, and he grinned reassuringly.

'It's all right, I'm not going to make things even more complicated than they are. I just want you to know—' he reached across to touch her hand '—I'm very fond of you, Libby. Given the chance, I could be a whole lot more. I think too much of Keir, and of you, to take advantage of the situation as it is now, but if ever you need anyone—' He stopped, but his meaning was clear and Libby felt a soft blush creep up into her cheeks. She had never dreamed that Jeremy could be feeling this way! In a way, it added to her own burdens, for here was someone else she could hurt, but she knew that Jeremy wasn't the sort to go head over heels. He was a more solid, reliable type than the passionate Keir; he would weigh up his own position before committing himself, and his emotions would be kept firmly in check until he was quite sure that they wouldn't be damaged.

That made him sound cold, she thought, and he wasn't that at all. He would be a passionate lover, a faithful husband. He might even be able to make her happy.

But that was something she couldn't even consider at this time, and Jeremy knew that. He was prepared to take a back seat, wait until—if ever—she was ready. Until then, he would be her friend.

'Thank you, Jeremy,' she said quietly, and he gave her an intent glance, then took his hand away, and she knew that the subject would not be mentioned again until she wanted it to be. She felt a warm wash of gratitude. And she felt a little less lonely than she had before.

Now she was standing inside the door of the dimly-lit flat, wondering just what had happened here during the day? Was Pia still here? Libby glanced around, looking for signs of the Italian girl's occupation, but there was none. Biting her lip, she tiptoed across the hall to the door of her own room. Now that she was here, she wanted to get to bed without having to meet or talk to anyone. Another scene now would be more than she could stand.

Her room looked just as it had when she had left it, and she put down her bag and kicked off the sandals she had been wearing all day. The tiles were cool to her bare feet and she thought longingly of a shower. Would it be safe to have one, or would she wake the others? Assuming, of course, that they were asleep! And if she did, would they come out to see where she had been? On the whole, it seemed unlikely. If Pia and Keir were enjoying their own reunion they wouldn't want to be disturbed any more than she wanted to disturb them. Neither of them was going to leave the other to come and talk to her—the interloper. She could walk around the flat naked for all they cared.

Her mind made up, Libby slipped out of her clothes and wrapped herself in a thin cotton housecoat. Just a quick shower, she promised herself, and went cautiously through to the bathroom. She hoped that there would be enough water for a shower—the Maltese supply was unpredictable and had been cut off twice already during her stay—but to her relief it sprayed almost with enthusiasm, at just the right temperature, and she stood underneath it, feeling it wash away her worries as well as the stickiness of the day, leaving her refreshed and strengthened by its pleasant coolness.

Rubbing her short hair into a fuzz of curls with a towel, she wrapped the housecoat around herself again, tying the belt loosely round her waist, and padded back to her bedroom. Obviously she had disturbed nobody; the flat was still silent. Keir and Pia must be asleep and she wouldn't have to face either of them until tomorrow. And then—she stopped just inside the door, a cry of surprise choking itself in her throat as she saw a dark figure sitting in the chair by the window.

'*Keir!*'

'Hullo, Libby,' he said equably. 'So you've come home at last?'

'Home?' Libby repeated, her voice trembling with shock. 'This isn't my home.'

Keir shrugged impatiently. 'A figure of speech.

Wherever I happen to be I call home. Especially,' he added, his voice soft as he got up and came towards her across the tiled floor, 'if you happen to be there, too.'

Libby gazed up at him. What did he mean? And where was Pia? Had he come fresh from her arms to Libby's room, or had she left the flat? A wild hope surged up inside her—had Pia given up so quickly, gone back to Italy without any fight at all?

Keir put out a lazy hand and caught at the belt that hung from Libby's waist. He pulled it gently, undoing the careless knot, and the cotton fell away from her body, revealing a provocative glimpse of bare skin underneath. Pulling a little harder, he drew her towards him.

'Keir,' she whispered, the betraying weakness flooding her body so that she was totally unable to resist. 'Keir, what's happened to Pia? Has she gone? Tell me, Keir.'

'Pia?' he murmured, his lips just touching hers with a butterfly caress that almost drove her wild. 'No, she hasn't gone, Libby. She's still here—in the flat—she—'

'She's *here*?' Libby jerked away from him. 'But—why aren't you with her? Why are you here—with me—'

'Why shouldn't I be?' he countered. 'I want to know where you've been all day, Libby. Why you ran out on me like that—just what game you're playing . . .'

'What game am *I* playing?' A small flare of anger came to Libby's rescue and she jerked herself out of his arms, hastily wrapping the gown around her and tying the belt with trembling fingers as she saw Keir's gaze on her slim body. '*You* weren't exactly bending over backwards to be helpful this morning. I just didn't know which way your mind was working. You didn't seem to mind her pawing you—what was I to think but that you were enjoying it? And I didn't much care for the idea of spending all day watching her do it.'

'So where did you go?' Keir's voice hardened as he rapped the question out, and Libby was faintly aware that he was in a volatile mood, still in a state of acute frustration which was as likely to turn to anger as to love.

'Is that any of your business?' she asked defiantly.

'I think it is, yes.'

Libby shrugged and turned away, determined not to let him see how afraid she was. 'If you must know, I went to Mellieha. Jeremy met me there and we—'

'Jeremy met you there? How did you get there?'

'On the bus, though I still don't see what—'

'And how did Jeremy know that was where you were going?' Keir demanded sceptically, a sneer in his voice.

'He used his brain, I suppose,' Libby snapped. 'Knew where the bus was going and followed it—*I* don't know! We didn't discuss it—'

'Because you didn't need to! Don't try to hide it, Libby . . . I've seen the way Jeremy looks at you. Another scalp for your belt, isn't he? Another poor fool you've conquered, like you conquered me. God help us both!'

'*No*—no, it's not like that at all!' Libby stopped abruptly, remembering Jeremy's words in the restaurant, and turned away as she felt her colour rise, and heard Keir give a snort of disbelief.

'I never thought you were that kind, Libby,' he said after a few moments, and his voice was quiet now in a different way; sadness had replaced the scorn and Libby felt an almost overwhelming desire to turn, throw her arms about him and tell him he was the only man she had loved or could ever love. But she stayed quite still, and heard him go on, each word like a knife to her heart. 'Maybe that's why we broke up—was it? Did you have other men when you'd sworn to love me, Libby? Was that what came between us?'

Libby shook her head. Her eyes were misted with tears. 'No, that wasn't the reason. Keir—please stop tormenting me like this. I—'

'*Tormenting* you?' His voice was like a whiplash now, the moment of sadness gone and the anger back. 'How can you talk of *me* tormenting *you*? You come here, letting me think that there's still a chance for us, you blow hot and cold all the time you are here, and then, when I really need you, you run off with my best friend and leave me not knowing whether you even intend to come back. And you say I'm tormenting you! Libby, you don't know what torment is, but by God, I've a damned good mind to show you!'

He grabbed her by both shoulders and jerked her round to face him. Libby felt a stab of panic as she looked up into his angry face. But she had no time to protest; his mouth was on hers, blotting out any cry she might have made, and his fingers were cruel on her body as they gripped her close against him. Her housecoat fell open again and she felt the hair of his thighs, his body naked apart from the shorts he had been wearing earlier, rough against her own smooth skin. With a sound deep in his throat, Keir shifted his grip, sliding his hands under the gown and over her skin, and Libby shuddered with a mixture of fear and desire as he pulled her against him, his sensuous movements telling her of his own arousal. He laid one arm along the small of her back, his kisses forcing her backwards so that she arched over, her head falling to expose her slim throat, and his lips moved down the taut column to the breast which was cupped in his other hand, the nipple stiffening as he took it between gently nipping teeth.

'You'll know what torment is by the time I've finished

with you,' he muttered, letting his hand roam more intimately over her arched body and ignoring the whimpering protest that was all she could make. 'You've made me suffer long enough, Libby—and that's just counting what I can remember! God knows what you did to me in the meantime! But if you think you can two-time me with *anyone*, let alone my best friend, you've got—'

'Keir, *no*!' Feebly, longing to submit but still held back by her mixed emotions, Libby struggled in his arms. 'It's *not* like that! And even if it were—' thankfully she dredged up that tiny flare of anger again '—even if it were, what business would it be of yours? Our engagement was broken two years ago, Keir. You don't have any rights over me, any at all. We're *not* engaged any more, can't you get that into your head? And we *can't* be, not until you get your memory back and know all about me—and about Pia!'

Keir's grip slackened for a moment and Libby wriggled away from him. She pulled the white gown about her again, feeling her heart like a hammer against her ribs, then pushed back her damp hair with a shaking hand. 'It's no use trying to settle it that way,' she told him, her voice roughened by tears that would not fall. 'You've got to accept the situation, Keir. It was all over between us two years ago. I don't know what's happened to you since then, and neither do you. But you don't have any say in what I do or who I see—can't you understand that?' He stared at her, saying nothing, and she added angrily: 'Your trouble is that you want both worlds—you want Pia, and you want me. But you can't have us both, Keir, and you've got to make a decision. It isn't fair on either of us!'

'And if I've made my decision?' he demanded. 'Doesn't that occur to you? Doesn't it occur to you that I haven't changed my mind at all—that it's still you, as it always has been, as it always will—'

'But it *hasn't* always been, has it? You lived with her, in Rome.'

The words were like ice in the warm air and Keir, momentarily defeated, turned away. Libby watched him tensely. If only Pia did not stand between them, how easy it would be to take him in her arms and tell him she loved him, needed him, wanted him. But Pia did stand between them. She was here in the flat—and Libby still did not know what had happened between Pia and Keir during the hours she had been away.

'Look—Libby—' Keir said, turning to her, his voice as taut as a bowstring, and Libby felt her muscles tighten, her nerves almost standing out from her flesh. 'I've got to tell you—'

But what he had to tell her, she never knew. For at that moment the bedroom door opened, and Pia stood there, tall and voluptuous in a black lace negligee that barely skimmed her rich figure, her white breasts swelling up from its plunging neckline, the bronze hair cascading on pale shoulders and violet eyes smouldering in the soft glow of the lamp.

Libby felt at the neck of her cotton housecoat, reflecting ruefully on the contrast she and the glamorous *contessa* must make. Her short hair was still damp from the shower, and she ran distracted fingers through it. God, hadn't she had enough for one day? And she couldn't even run away and leave them—not when they were in her own bedroom!

'So this is where you are, *caro*,' Pia drawled, the fluid Italian accent soft in her throat. 'I woke and you were not there . . .' The implication was obvious and Libby felt bitterness like nausea in her mouth. 'So the wanderer has returned.' The violet eyes flickered over

Libby, taking in the simple housecoat and the slender, almost boyish figure. 'Was there something you wanted, little one?'

'Nothing,' Libby answered coldly, keeping her eyes away from Keir. 'Just a good night's rest, if you don't mind.'

'And I am sure Keir is only too pleased to see that you have it.' Pia walked across to Keir and slid her arm through his. 'Such a good host, are you not, *caro*?' she murmured. 'Even the inconsiderate guest is looked after so well, no? But you can see that the little one wants only to sleep so come with me, and let us all do the same.'

Keir glanced down at her, his eyes masked. Then he seemed to come to life. He pulled his arm firmly away from her and put her gently to one side. Then, ignoring the sudden anger of the purple eyes, he moved across the room to Libby and laid his hand on her shoulder.

'You just won't take telling, will you, Pia?' he said, his voice hard. 'God knows I've tried to break it gently today, but you just don't want to listen. So here it is, straight. *Libby* is the girl I love—the girl I want to marry. And she loves me too, though she tries not to show it. So far you've stood in our way, but not any longer.' He turned to Libby, looked down into her eyes and the emotion in his own was naked, no longer masked, no longer hidden. It blazed out of him and she caught her breath, realising that she could stand against it no longer. Whatever else might happen, this was genuine, and if she hadn't seen it before, she must have been blind.

'You will marry me, won't you, Libby?' he demanded urgently. 'For God's sake say yes—say it now. Stop this hell we've both been living in and make Pia see the truth—or else leave me. Because I can't take any more of this, I swear I can't!'

Libby stared up at him, hypnotised by the burning

eyes. She could see now that every word he spoke was true. He did love her—whatever had happened in between. And that love had endured, lived through two years of separation, survived an accident that had left a great hole in his life. He might never remember what had happened during that time, but it no longer mattered. They belonged together and no more time must be wasted.

'Yes, Keir,' she whispered, not caring that Pia stood looking on with furious, jealous eyes. 'Yes, I'll marry you—tomorrow if you like. Oh, Keir—' But she wasn't allowed to get any further. The Italian girl, shaking with rage now, her eyes huge pools of malevolence in her ashen face, stepped forward, her jaw thrust out, her hands clenched into angry fists.

'Marry?' she rasped, and her voice was ugly now. 'Keir, what nonsense is this? Are you hoping to make me jealous? You cannot really mean this ridiculous proposal—not after what that girl did to you?' They both turned to look at her. 'Oh yes, I know all about it!' she went on, her voice shrilling through the room. 'Do you imagine that he never told me? We were close—there were no secrets between us! Yes, I know all about it—all about your infidelity, your perfidy!'

'You do?' Keir said grimly, while Libby clung to him, shivering with fear that even now Pia might split them apart with lies. 'Then let me hear it.'

'Oh no.' Pia attempted a return to her old seductive drawl. 'Not here, *caro*—in private. Where this one cannot interrupt with her lies—'

'Leaving you free to tell yours,' Keir commented. 'It's no use, Pia. We've had all day together and I can see that you might have satisfied my—appetite—once. It's clear that it was your appetite too. But love—no. We would never have got within a mile of love, you and I. And now that I've found the girl I really did love—' his arm tightened about Libby's shoulders. '—I'm afraid anything we had is over. I did tell you I'd been trying to break it gently,' he added quietly.

Pia stood quite still. She looked from one to the other and Libby saw that although her magnificent chest still heaved with anger, she was controlling it. But there was no disguising the spite that still flickered in her eyes, and when she spoke her voice was sharp with malice.

'So there is nothing else for it,' she said in brittle tones. 'You will have to know it all. I had meant to tell you this in a different way, Keir, *caro mio*. When we were alone—perhaps when we were warm and contented after love. But the occasion has not arisen, and now you must know in a less romantic way.' There was triumph in the glance she flicked at Libby then. 'You will not leave me and marry this little English miss, Keir. I can tell you that. You will not even think of it. Because if you do, you will be abandoning not only me, but your child. *Your own child*—your son, perhaps, or your daughter. And I think that you are not the man to do such a thing—am I right?' The triumph was blazing in her face now, and Libby felt a coldness creep over her body, turning her heart to ice. 'Yes, Keir, I am carrying a child—*your* child—and I intend that it should have its own father. Can you really deny that?'

CHAPTER EIGHT

THE silence was absolute. Libby backed away and sank down on her bed, cold with horror. Keir and Pia stared at each other; Pia with gloating victory, Keir with a sick, shocked whiteness.

'Well?' Pia challenged him. 'Are you ready to deny your son? For I am sure it will be a son, Keir. A son made from our love,' she added caressingly, and Libby turned her face away.

'How—how far—' Keir began huskily, and Pia smiled.

'I am just over three months pregnant. Oh yes, it is quite certain—you may have a doctor's confirmation if you wish, but time will soon begin to tell. There is no doubt about it, Keir, none at all.'

'And how long have you known?'

Pia shrugged. 'For six, seven weeks I have been certain. You are wondering why I did not come to tell you the good news at once—or at least write, or phone. But all was not so easy, Keir. For one thing, I was not entirely sure of my own feelings.' The violet eyes taunted him. 'It is a serious thing for a woman, you realise—marriage. I had to decide whether I wanted you to be the father of my child.'

A deliberate barb to rouse Keir's pride, Libby thought hopelessly, and it seemed to have worked. Keir's tanned face flushed and his eyes glittered. But he spoke calmly enough.

'And you decided eventually in my favour.'

'But of course.' Again that eloquent shrug. 'There

really wasn't much doubt, was there? Not after the time we had together . . . But I found those early weeks trying, Keir. You know—the sickness on rising, the tiredness. I did not want to travel feeling so, and I did not wish to come to you in such a condition. Now—she held out her hands. '—I am full of life again—in truth, yes?'

Keir turned away. His shoulders were bowed and Libby, watching him, knew that this was defeat. Pia had played her trump card, and it had proved to be an ace. There was no way they could get around this.

'Well, Keir?' Pia said softly.

Keir's voice was ragged. 'We'll talk about it in the morning. I need time to think—we all do.'

'*I* need no time,' Pia said. 'I have had plenty. But if that is your wish—' She could afford to be magnanimous, Libby thought, knowing that she had won. 'So, we will meet for breakfast, yes? And you—' The beautiful eyes flashed venom at Libby '—you may as well begin to pack now. You must surely see that there is nothing—nothing whatever for you here.'

Libby didn't answer—she couldn't. Her throat ached and she wanted nothing more than to crawl into her bed and sleep, forgetting this nightmare. Oh, if only it *were* a nightmare, she thought despairingly. If only she could wake up in her own flat in London, with all this a jumbled figment of her imagination. But it was all too real, and she knew quite well that it would still be going on tomorrow. And the next day, and the next, and the next . . .

She looked up to find Keir's eyes fixed on her, and knew that he was begging for her help. But there was nothing she could do. Things had gone beyond her now—this situation was between him and Pia and was nothing to do with her any more. There could be no more comforting, no more promises.

Pia was right. She might as well start packing now. There was nothing for her on Malta any more. Nothing.

Libby was up early next morning. She had slept very little and her eyes looked bruised as she quickly packed her bags. During the dark, endless night her thoughts had whirled about her brain until she thought she would go mad. But by the time the grey dawn had crept through the unshuttered windows, bringing the room into a vague shape again, she had come to a decision.

As Pia had said, she might as well go at once. Only Keir could cope with the situation now, and Libby's continued presence could only be a distraction. And could only mean added pain for both Keir and herself.

The bells of the church had just begun to ring for six o'clock Mass as she slipped out of the quiet flat. Presumably Pia and Keir were still sleeping—apart, from what had been said. And she gave Keir a mental apology for her thoughts about him and the *contessa* yesterday. Apparently, he had *not* succumbed to her charms, and Libby had wronged him in thinking that he would.

Not that it made any difference now. Pia must have known all the time that she would win—she had been just playing them along, as a cat does a mouse, tormenting them by letting them get a little way away, then jerking them back, and repeating the exercise for her own amusement before making the final kill.

Libby set her cases down at the corner of the street, wondering what to do next. It was too early for a bus or a taxi, and she didn't much fancy wandering the streets of Zurrieq with her luggage, under the curious eyes of the Maltese. And at any time, Keir might discover her absence and come after her.

Jeremy! He had a room at the edge of the village—he had pointed out the house to her once. And she needn't worry about waking the household, most people were up and about by now and there were already women coming back from the shops with fresh bread or gathering round the vans and carts that brought vegetables, fruit and fish to their doors every morning.

Picking up her luggage again, Libby walked through the twisting alleys, through the square and past the *Armeria*, where several of the grandmasters had kept weapons to supply the surrounding villages. She plunged into the maze of streets on the other side and eventually, after several rests and two or three wrong turns, found the house where Jeremy was lodging.

Yes, he was in, the plump Maltese woman told her, her eyes bright with interest as she glanced past Libby at the luggage behind her. Perhaps the lady would like to come inside and rest while she told Mr Brooke he had a visitor.

Libby sat down thankfully and waited. Jeremy had never been known for early rising, she remembered, and it was several minutes before he appeared looking as if he had hastily dipped his head in a bowl of cold water and scrambled into the first pair of shorts and shirt he had come to. At least he didn't have to shave!

'Libby?' Jeremy's brown eyes were anxious. 'What's happened?' he saw her cases and his eyebrows shot up. 'What is it?'

'I'm leaving,' Libby said baldly, and her eyes filled with tears.

Jeremy scooped her up into his arms. He held her close and she let her head drop on to his chest while she wept, feeling the tears that had been building up through all the sleepless, dry-eyed night, flow like a suddenly undammed river. She was conscious of Jeremy's arms, warm and strong around her, aware of his hand stroking her short hair, and she remembered what he had said yesterday in Mellieha. He would stand by her, she knew, but as no more than a friend—she had to make that clear. Her emotions were too badly bruised to let her think of love again, ever.

'Tell me what's happened,' Jeremy said at last in a gentle voice, and she lifted her face and wiped her streaming eyes with the hanky he gave her.

'Pia's pregnant,' she told him. 'She told Keir last night—after I arrived. She's carrying Keir's child, Jeremy, and there's nothing anyone can do about it.'

Jeremy whistled. '*Pregnant!* Are you sure—sure it's true?'

Libby shrugged. 'She says she'll have a medical examination if Keir doesn't believe her. Anyway, she's three months—it would start to show in a few weeks. I don't think there's any doubt about it, Jeremy.'

Jeremy sucked in his top lip. 'No wonder you want to leave.' He moved away from her as his landlady came in with a tray of coffee. 'Here, have a hot drink. You look as though you need it. Then we'll give this matter some thought.' He poured Libby a large cup of coffee, which she accepted gratefully, then made her a thick ham sandwich which she couldn't eat.

'There's nothing to think about,' she said. 'It's all over as far as I'm concerned, Jeremy. Pia means to marry Keir and she's holding all the cards now. All I can do is get out of the way—maybe it'll be easier for him then.'

Jeremy sighed. 'It's all wrong, Libby. Pia was never the woman for Keir, and you are. You're leaving him to a life of misery.'

'And what else can I do?' she asked with a flash of anger. 'It isn't just Keir we have to think about now. There's a child—*his* child. He's not even denying it, Jeremy. He'll have to marry her.'

'Will he? Do people have shotgun marriages these days?'

'Not in England, perhaps,' Libby said quietly. 'But Pia isn't English. She's Italian—and that makes a difference.'

'A shotgun marriage—and no divorce.' Jeremy shook his head. 'It's a hell of a decision, Libby.'

'But it's not my decision,' she reminded him. 'And it's a decision that was really made three months ago. It might even have been deliberate—On Keir's part as much as on Pia's.'

'I don't believe that!' Jeremy exclaimed, but there was a tinge of doubt in his voice.

Libby took a drink of coffee, feeling the hot liquid warm and comfort her shivering body a little. 'There's really nothing to discuss, is there?' she said. 'I just came to you for transport really, Jeremy. Will you take me to the airport? I'd like to go back to London as soon as possible, before—' Her voice broke and Jeremy put his hand on her shoulder.

'Yes, of course I will,' he said soberly. 'And I'm damned sorry it's turned out this way. I hoped—well, you know what I hoped.' He paused. 'This probably isn't the time to say it, but I may not get another chance. Remember what I told you yesterday—I'm here if you want me. Any time—just let me know. Remember that, won't you?'

'I'll remember,' Libby said, and smiled up at him tremulously.

'Now,' he said, finishing the sandwich that Libby had left on her plate, 'you really are determined to go back to London straight away?'

'Yes. It's the only thing I can do.' Libby looked at him, her eyes the colour of clouds. 'Will I be able to get a flight, do you think?'

'Well, we'll have to see.' He glanced at his watch. 'I'll phone the airport right away. I should think there'll be something, but you never know, sometimes the flights are pretty full.'

He went out of the room, leaving Libby with some fresh coffee, and she could hear him using the telephone in another room. She wondered if Keir were awake yet, if he had discovered her absence. Surely he wouldn't follow her—he must realise this was the only action she could take. And she didn't believe that he would refuse to marry Pia, not if she was expecting his child. Keir was a man of powerful integrity—she remembered his own care for her during their engagement—and that was something that wouldn't have changed.

Libby sighed and gazed out of the window at the narrow street. A line of poetry had come to her mind during the night—what was it? Something from Shakespeare, something she remembered from school '. . . memory, a rooted sorrow . . .' Memory had certainly proved a 'rooted sorrow' for Keir and for herself, with complications that no one could have foreseen.

Jeremy came back, frowning a little, and her heart sank. Hadn't he been able to book a seat for her after all? Her eyes questioned him, and he shook his head ruefully.

'Nothing until tomorrow, I'm afraid,' he reported. 'A lot of people have been taking late holidays—maybe it's school half-term or something. But I'm afraid it means you have to stay on Malta for another day.'

Libby bit her lip. 'And this is one of the first places Keir will look,' she said. 'At least—I hope he *won't* look for me. But I'm afraid he will.'

'I think so, too.' Jeremy thought for a moment. 'We'll have to find you somewhere else to stay. Where do you think will be best?'

Libby shrugged. 'I suppose Valletta—it's the most crowded. Or Rabat.' She thought wistfully of the peace of Mdina. 'I don't really care, Jeremy. I just want to keep out of Keir's way.'

'And I'm not keen on leaving you alone.' Jeremy looked at her. 'Well, I don't suppose Keir will be wanting me today. I'll come with you and we'll have a tour round some of Malta's remoter spots. It'll pass the time, if nothing else. You can stay somewhere in Valletta for the night and I'll take you to the airport tomorrow. That suit you?'

'I suppose it will have to,' Libby sighed. A day's sightseeing, with the risk of running into Keir at any time, was the last thing she needed just now. Then she realised how ungracious she sounded and gave Jeremy a rueful smile. 'Yes, it will be fine, Jeremy. I'm really grateful to you. This isn't easy for you either, is it?'

'Not so as you'd notice, no. But I'm on the outside—I just wish I could do more to help.' He sighed again. 'I wish I hadn't left Keir in Rome to go to London and come on here. It means that Pia is the only person who knows just what happened in those weeks—it puts her in altogether too strong a position.'

'I don't see that it would have made any difference,' Libby said pessimistically. 'You still couldn't have prevented what happened.'

'No . . . all the same . . .' Jeremy frowned, as if trying to remember something. Then he obviously dismissed whatever it was from his mind and gave Libby a determined grin. 'Well, if you're ready, we'll go. I'll just load your bags into Bertie—hope he can stand the strain—and we won't need to come back here. Wouldn't do to find Keir lying in wait for us when we got back this evening!'

'No. Though I don't see why he should. He must know there's nothing else to be done.' Libby followed Jeremy out to the pavement, where his battered little car seemed to be leaning against the kerb as if gathering strength for the day ahead. She looked at it with some sympathy; in both her mind and her emotions she felt no less battered, and just as much in need of strength.

The day passed by in a steady assault on the island's sights. Libby saw it all through a blur and could never afterwards remember the exact order in which they covered ground. When she tried, it was like watching a travel film that was run too fast—a flickering panorama of soaring cliffs where they ate lunch looking down on a green and fertile valley before the final sheer drop to the sea; of watching fishermen, balanced hundreds of feet above the foaming waves, casually leaning out to drop their lines into the water; of sunlit streets where women sat at their doors making lace with rapid fingers, and darkened catacombs where once burials were carried out and people hid from the bombers that brought death from the skies.

If Jeremy had set out with the intention of giving her no time to think, he had every right to succeed, but nothing could stop the thoughts that teemed in Libby's brain, nothing could blot out her images of Keir. She thought of him constantly—his tall, lean figure, the way his hair, bleached by the sun, blew in the wind, the deep, glittering blue of his eyes. And his hands; those long, sensitive fingers that knew just where to touch her to turn her to jelly in his arms, have her crying out for the completion of their love. How many opportunities she had missed, she thought regretfully, and now they would never come again. And she wished bitterly that she had not drawn back, that she had answered the clamour of Keir's body and her own. At least she would have had his love; she would have the experience to remember, to carry with her. Now, she had nothing.

At last it was time to return to Valletta and the hotel where Jeremy had booked her in for the night. Dazed and tired out by the day, following a sleepless night and an equally stressful day, Libby refused Jeremy's offer of dinner. She would have something in her room, she told him, and get a good night's sleep. And she would see him tomorrow, when he came to take her to the airport.

'I won't forget this, Jeremy,' she said as they stood in the quiet corridor outside her room. 'I don't know how I would have coped without you.'

Jeremy grunted, and she knew that he didn't want her thanks or her gratitude, but something far deeper—something she couldn't give him, would probably never be able to give him. She gave a little sigh, thinking how sad and how complicated life could be. Yet people did manage to live simple, happy lives—her sister Claire, for instance, with her husband Simon and the twin boys who were now almost two years old. Why couldn't it happen to Libby as it had happened to Claire?

She watched Jeremy go away down the corridor and went into her room. The window overlooked the Grand Harbour and she stood by it for a while, watching the twinkling lights reflected in the water. The gaily-coloured water-taxis—*dghajsa*—with their high prows painted with the eye of Osiris to keep devils away, were still moving about and she could hear the clop of hooves from the horse-drawn *karrozzin* as they carried tourists around, showing them the points of interest of the city. And above, around and between all this came the hubbub of voices as Maltese and visitors alike paraded the streets.

Libby felt suddenly restless. Tired as she was, she knew that she would not be able to sleep—and if she did, she would only wake again to lie in the loneliness of night until dawn came. Better to go out now, walk until she could be sure of sleep at a later hour.

She picked up a light jacket and slung it over her shoulder. The air was mild, but she had noticed in the past day or two that there could be a chilly breeze; a taste of winter, though winter in Malta was a milder affair altogether than at home. Still, November was almost here and one had to expect a cooling in the weather.

Outside, she hesitated, unsure of where to go. Keir had brought her to Valletta since their first visit, but she still didn't know the streets very well—their visits had been mainly to look at historical sites. She remembered the morning they had spent in the War Museum, a heartbreaking picture of the sufferings of the island during its bombardment. Keir certainly had plenty of material here for his book, she thought, and wished that she could have shared more of its preparation with him.

Deep in thought, she wandered unseeingly through the streets bustling with people. And when she realised that she was, after all, hungry, it seemed almost inevitable that she should find herself standing outside the restaurant where she and Keir had eaten on that first evening.

Such a long time ago, she thought, looking up at it. I had no idea then what was wrong—why Keir had written to me, begging me to come. If I had—would I have stayed? If I could have looked into the future, would I have drawn back then, gone home without giving it a chance? Or would I have done just the same . . . in the hope that things just might turn out differently?

There was no knowing. But she went into the restaurant as if drawn by a magnet. It would be her last link with Keir, she thought as she was shown to the same table where they had sat and looked out at the darkened water, the tiny points of light, the glow of the reflections. Just for an hour, she would sit here and pretend—pretend that they were together, that nothing could come between them. And then she would go back to her lonely hotel room, and tomorrow she would go back to London. And then . . . ? She shook the question away. She would face that later.

It was only as she started to drink her coffee, having refused a dessert, that she glanced again at the window. This time, instead of looking through at the darkness outside, her attention was caught by the reflection. She saw the restaurant's interior, dim and mysterious as rooms always are when seen as reflections; she saw herself, pale and large-eyed, lifting the cup to her lips. And, behind her, she saw a reflection of Keir himself, standing quite still, watching her in the glass.

I'm going mad, she thought. I've cracked at last, and now I'm hallucinating. Conjuring up visions. Oh, what's happening to me? And she set her cup down and leaned her head on her hand.

'Don't worry, Libby,' Keir's voice came as he laid a hand on her shoulder and came round the table to sit opposite her. 'It really is me. You don't shake me off quite so easily, you know.'

Libby lifted her face and stared at him with eyes that were like pools of rain in her pale face.

'What are you doing here?' she whispered. 'Why have you come—how did you find me?'

'I won't even bother to answer that first question,' he said harshly, and she saw now that his face was tight with repressed anger, his lips a thin line in a rigid jaw. 'Or even the second. As to how I found you, it wasn't too hard. I guessed you meant to go back to London, so the airport was my first concern. You hadn't left today, but they had a reservation for you for tomorrow. It was pretty obvious that you'd stay somewhere nearby and Valletta was the likeliest place. So I rang round the hotels until I found out where you were. And when I found that you'd booked in and gone out—alone—I just thought it might be a chance that you'd come here.'

Libby looked at him. It hadn't been by choice that she had come here—or had it? Had some subconscious hope or desire led her to this place, where she had been with Keir?

'I'll have a few words to say to Master Jeremy when I see him, all the same,' Keir continued grimly. 'I imagine he's been with you in all this.'

Libby spread her hands helplessly. 'It wasn't his fault, Keir. I asked him to help me—he didn't want to go against you, but there was nothing else I could do.'

'That remains to be seen. You didn't stay to see if there was a chance, did you? Just up and ran—wasn't very brave, was it, Libby?'

'And was there any reason why I should be *brave*?' Libby countered hotly. 'It's a pretty clear-cut case, isn't it? You were Pia's lover and you're the father of her child—what place do I have in that situation? An ex-fiancée whom you hadn't seen or contacted for two years? What was there to be brave about? You need me around like your need a hole in the head,' she finished bitterly, 'and when that plane leaves for London tomorrow I'm going to be on it.'

'I suppose you wish you'd never come here,' Keir said in a low voice, and suddenly Libby saw the only way in which she could make him let her leave. She had to make him believe that she no longer loved him,.even though she longed even now to take him in her arms, kiss away the lines that scored his haggard face. It wasn't *his* fault all this had happened, she told herself, but that wasn't the point. It *had* happened, and there was only one path he could take, and they both knew it.

'Yes, I do wish I'd never come,' she said, endeavouring to keep her voice steady. 'Because as far as I'm concerned it's all been just one big waste of time. You aren't the man I thought you were, Keir. You're nothing but a womaniser, taking love—if you can call it that—where you find it, regardless of the consequences, regardless of who gets hurt. Well, now there have been consequences you can't ignore. There's a baby on the way, Keir, and it's yours. God knows what kind of a father you'll be, but if you're worth anything you'll do the best you can for that child. Because it's the only innocent, truly innocent, party in this whole sorry mess, and it's up to you to make up to it for what seems to me to be a pretty poor beginning.' She got up from the table, picking up her bag and jacket, and summoned up all the scorn she could muster as she looked down at him. 'Don't follow me out, Keir. I'd rather be on my own.'

'And this is just one time when you don't get what you want,' Keir gritted as he thrust back his chair and reached out hard fingers for her arm. 'And don't go rushing off without paying your bill—that *would* be embarrassing.'

Libby threw him a glance of sheer hatred as she halted. How *could* she have forgotten that she hadn't yet paid? And now she had to wait, trying to look pleasant and assured, while the waiter made out her bill and handed it to her, clearly puzzled by the situation and almost giving it to Keir instead. But Keir just stood there, impassive, making it quite clear that this time the lady paid. And that certainly was what she was doing now, Libby thought bitterly as she left the change on the plate and set off once again for the door. If anyone was paying for all this, she was. And she made a mental note to tell Sally that she had been quite right—she was utterly and completely mad to have come to Malta.

At least the little incident had had the effect of making her really angry with Keir, and that could only be a help. Perhaps now they could have a real show down and she could go back to England angry rather than unhappy. In any case, she wasn't making any more allowances for his amnesia. He had been treated like an invalid long enough, she thought, and from now on it was no holds barred.

'Right,' Keir said tersely when they were out in the street. 'Let's go somewhere where we can talk without being interrupted. I suggest your hotel room.'

'Oh—no—' Libby began, but he ignored her protest and wheeled round, his fingers still like an iron bracelet round her arm, and set off along the road. Libby was half-dragged along, her feet slipping and sliding in their high-heeled sandals, but it was clear that any resistance would be useless. Numb with fear, she let him jerk her through the double doors into the foyer and in a low voice she asked for her key. They went to the lift in silence, watched by the dark eyes of the receptionist.

Keir took the key from Libby and opened her door. He closed it behind them, locked it again and slipped the key into his pocket.

'Right,' he said pleasantly, 'and now what about a nice long talk?'

'There's nothing to talk about,' Libby said tonelessly. 'The facts are quite clear, whether you acknowledge them or not. Our engagement was broken off two years ago. You've lived with another woman since then and she's expecting your child. There's nothing to be done about that, and all I want to do is get home and forget the whole sorry mess.'

'And you think you'll be able to do that?'

Libby shrugged. 'I'll have to.'

The sapphire eyes met hers with a look that seemed to burn right through to her brain. She felt her colour rise and turned away. Had Keir always known her so well, or was this something recent—something that had developed during their separation, perhaps through his own experiences?

'You may try,' Keir said then, very softly, 'but you'll never be able to. Never!' His tone hardened on the last word and he stepped forward, reaching for her, but Libby backed away swiftly, hands upraised, and he checked. 'You see—you can't risk my touching you even now. Because your body knows the truth, doesn't it, Libby. Every cell of your body knows that we belong together, you and I. That whatever happened two years ago, whatever's happened since, none of it has made the slightest difference. We were meant to be together—or why would you be here now?'

'I—don't know,' Libby said shakily. 'I must have been mad to come, I—'

'You weren't mad,' he told her. 'In fact, it was probably the first sane thing you've done in two years. You read that letter and you knew what you had to do. You knew I needed you—and you knew too that you needed me. Isn't that right?'

The last question cracked through the room like a pistol shot, and Libby put up her hands again in self-defence. But Keir didn't approach her again; he stood where he was, watching her closely, and she felt uncertainty catch at her heart. Yes, it was right, but did she have to admit it? Wouldn't that be her undoing? She shook her head wildly.

'No—no, it's not right! I didn't know any such thing. I just—I just—' She struggled for words, seeing Keir's sardonic eyes on her, hating him more at every moment. 'I just needed to find out, I—'

'Find out—find out what?'

'Oh, I don't know—' Libby put her hands to her head. 'Stop rapping these questions at me, Keir—I can't think any more, I don't know what I mean any more. Oh, why can't you leave me alone? Why?'

'You know that as well as I do,' he said quietly, and now he did come forward and place his hands on her arms—not cruelly any more, but gently, firmly. 'And we also both know what it is you came to find out. Don't we? *Don't* we?' He gave her a tiny shake and her head came up so that her eyes met his. They weren't angry any more, she noticed remotely; they were dark and filled with emotion, and the look in them twisted her suffering heart.

'You came to find out whether it was still there—what we had two years ago,' Keir stated. 'That's the truth, isn't it, Libby? Oh, you've tried to forget me, I don't doubt that—you've tried to push me out of your mind, pretend I never existed, start what you probably called a new life. You did all that—just as I did, turning to other women who never seemed to have that elusive quality that only you have for me. It didn't work for me and I don't think it worked for you. So when you got my letter, you came—to find out if we could go back. Answer me, Libby—isn't that right?'

His voice wasn't harsh any more. Libby bit her lip. She still couldn't bring herself to say the words—she was too afraid of what might happen. But Keir wasn't going to let her get away with it. His fingers moved on her arms, reminding her of the power and the magic that he possessed over her, and his eyes looked at her with an intentness she couldn't avoid.

'Say it, Libby,' he commanded. 'You have to say

it—for your own sake as well as for mine. You'll never know any peace if you don't.'

Mesmerised by that look, aware suddenly of a strange confidence that she couldn't analyse, Libby knew that he was right. She had to say it. Whatever came next—whatever was going to happen—she couldn't deny her real feelings any longer. For a moment, she veiled her eyes with sooty lashes as she gathered her courage, just as if she were a high-diver preparing for the biggest plunge of her life. Then, in acknowledgment that this was to be the truth, she raised her glance to his and said quietly:

'Yes, Keir. You're right. I came because I needed to know what—if anything—there still was between us. From your letter, it seemed as if you thought there might be something. I had to see you to find out. It was the only way to know if it was real.'

'And when you came?'

'I found out,' she whispered. 'I found that I loved you, Keir. I suppose I never really stopped.'

He jerked her towards him then as if he couldn't help himself, clasping her against his body as kisses found their way into her tousled hair, her ears, the curve of her neck. Libby's heart kicked at her breast; she held him, straining close, lifting her face for his kisses, tears salting their lips. For the first time since she had come to Malta she felt that the bond between them had been fully restored, never really broken. It had always been there, waiting. The love they had shared was as strong, as powerful, as magical as ever . . .

Only now it was impossible. And she broke away, tears raining down her cheeks as she stumbled to the window, stricken with grief that the only love she had ever found, ever wanted, couldn't come true.

Keir came behind her, laying his hands gently on her

shoulders. This time, Libby didn't break away. There was no threat in his touch any more, no danger. She let her head drop back to rest against his chest, and felt the strong beating of his heart against her ear.

'It's all right, Libby,' he breathed. 'I'm not going to force you to do anything you don't want. But we had to get it out in the open, don't you see? We had to have the truth between us, or it would all have been unbearable.'

'It's unbearable anyway,' she said in a muffled voice. 'There's nothing we can do about it, Keir. Pia's claim has to come first. You've got to let me go.'

'Not Pia's claim,' he said grimly. 'The child's. That's all that counts with me as far as she's concerned.' He lifted one hand and ran the fingers through his blond hair. 'Libby, you've got to believe me—I may not remember what happened between me and Pia, but I know myself well enough to be sure it was never more than an affair. I could never have loved her. As for the baby—' he shrugged '—God knows how that happened. I've never risked such a thing—but how can I say why it had to happen this time?' His jaw tightened. 'I can only think that it was Pia's doing—that she intended to trap me all along, and finally succeeded.'

'But it's still your child,' Libby said, and he nodded.

'Oh yes. It's still my child.'

They stood silently, close together, for a few moments. Libby saw without really registering the reflections in the dark water, the lights across the harbour. A romantic scene—a scene many couples must have watched as they stood here before going to bed. Honeymoon couples, couples long-married; couples whose lives were uncomplicated, who had every right to be here together, who could let the romance sweep them away to a world beyond the stars.

'So what happens now?' she asked. 'I can't stay

with you, Keir. You're not asking me to do that, are you?'

He slid his arm around her, holding her tightly against him, and she shivered.

'No, I'm not asking you to do that. It would go against all your instincts, all your principles, and no good could come of that.' He made a small, rueful noise, almost a chuckle. 'Blast it, it goes against mine too! But one day—' his arm tightened again '—one day things may come right. Do I have the right to ask you to wait, Libby? I'm not sure that I do.'

Libby moved helplessly in his arms. 'I don't know, Keir. How can things possibly come right? Pia's Italian—she'll never agree to a divorce. And you can't possibly marry her with the intention of asking her to. And the baby—you can't desert it now, how could you later? No, Keir—we can't live on that hope, it would be wrong.' She turned impulsively. 'Let me go, Keir,' she begged, her face against his chest. 'Let me go and forget me—it's the only way.'

There was a long silence as they clung together. Then Keir, his voice ragged with emotion, muttered: 'If I do that, will you stop loving me? I could bear it if I knew that somewhere you loved me.'

'I'll always love you. I'll never stop now.'

He heaved a great sigh; then, reluctantly, he released her. Libby stood still, slender and pale against the window, watching him almost unbelievingly as he walked to the door. She wanted to run after him, to throw her arms around him, to beg him to stay, to hold her, to give her one last kiss. But she knew that even Keir's iron self-control could only stand so much; no more. She bit her lip hard and watched without moving or speaking as he unlocked the door, gave her one last burning glance, and walked out.

Then she flung herself on the bed and let the tears of loss and grief fall as they would.

There was no sunshine when Libby woke next morning. The sky was grey with lumpy clouds, their darkness accentuated by the few glimpses of blue sky between them. She remembered that this was the beginning of the rainy season and that the weather had, in fact, been unusually settled for October. It looked as if it were about to break now.

Well, that was appropriate enough. It wasn't the only thing to break—her heart felt as if it were in smithereens, a shattered pile of fragments. Too many ever to be mended as one clean break might have been.

Feeling that all the colour had gone out of life, Libby dressed, drank some coffee and got ready for the drive to the airport. Jeremy had arranged to collect her in good time, and she had a moment's panic, wondering if Keir might come in his place. Oh no, please not, she prayed—it had been bad enough last night, she just didn't have the strength to part from him if he came this morning. But to her relief, when she went down to the foyer it was Jeremy who waited there, his bulky body and shaggy beard reassuringly familiar, his brown eyes kind and concerned.

Libby gave him her bags and turned to the desk to pay her bill. She had to wait a few minutes as other guests were attended to; then there was only one before her, a tall, slim man with dark hair and a small, pointed beard, and while he was talking to the receptionist she got out her money and passport.

'Yes, that is right,' the man was saying, and the familiarity of his accent made her look up suddenly. 'Raffaello Volturno. I booked in yesterday. I don't know how long I shall be staying.'

Libby watched him, puzzling a little over the accent—why should it sound familiar to her? Then another receptionist arrived and she shrugged—why should it matter to her anyway? Didn't she have more to worry about on this grey overcast morning than the accent of a stranger she was never going to see again?

Jeremy came in just as she left the desk, and they went out to the car together. Poor little battered, Beat-up Bertie, Libby thought with affection. How long would it be before it fell apart, just as her own life had fallen apart? But she shook herself then—self-pity wasn't going to help at all. Somehow, during the flight back home, she had to pull herself together—think what she was going to do next. Because telling Keir she loved him, feeling secure at last in his love for her, hadn't solved any of her practical problems. She still had to decide how to spend the rest of her life.

'Well, this is it,' Jeremy said as they arrived at the airport and he parked the car. 'Your last chance to look on Malta. I'm afraid it's been rather a strain, this visit. You haven't got much out of it, really, have you?'

'Not a lot,' Libby agreed, trying to smile. Only that I know Keir loves me, she thought sadly. Only that I know it can never come right. She laid her hand on Jeremy's arm. 'I *have* made a friend,' she said quietly. 'And friends are always worth making.'

'Well, maybe that's some compensation,' he said lightly, but his eyes were grave. 'Libby—we'll keep in touch, won't we?'

Libby hesitated. Would it be a good idea? Did she really want news of Keir coming through his closest friend, a man who would presumably continue to accompany him on his travels, know him better than anyone? Then she caught Jeremy's anxious glance and reproached herself. Jeremy had made it quite clear that he could feel more than ordinary friendship for her—he had helped her nevertheless, putting his own feelings second—how could she tell him she didn't want to keep in touch with him? 'Of course we will,' she said warmly. 'And thanks for everything, Jeremy. It would all have been much worse if you hadn't been here.'

Jeremy muttered something she couldn't catch, then looked up as her flight was announced. With a quick movement, he bent his head. As the crowd surged around them on the way to the flight gate, he kissed her; then he let her go and, half-blinded by sudden tears, she picked up her bags and stumbled away.

When she had found her seat at last and looked out for her last glimpse of the strange, historic island where an essential part of her own life had been played out, she could see the little car, Beat-up Bertie, standing on the hot tarmac. Jeremy was standing beside it, his beard a shadow in the sun that had just flickered out for a moment before the rain began. And beside him stood someone else: a man who was tall and lean, whose hair glinted like newly-ripened corn, whose dark blue eyes, even at this distance, seemed to look straight into hers.

He couldn't really see her. But Libby lifted her hand all the same, laid her lips on it and then held it against the window. Nobody could deny her that gesture of love; it would, after all, be the last one she ever made.

CHAPTER NINE

It was a good deal colder on Dartmoor than in Malta, Libby thought as she wrapped herself in an old sheepskin jacket and went downstairs. Claire was in the hall, buttoning the twins into their winter coats, and she looked up with a smile as her sister stopped beside them.

'Are you sure you don't mind taking them out?' she asked. 'It really isn't a very nice afternoon, but they ought to have some exercise and they love the Meadows. Or were you thinking of going on to the moor?'

'Moor, moor!' the twins chanted, and Libby gave them a rueful glance.

'Doesn't seem as if I have much choice, does it? I hope it won't be too cold for them up there.'

'Well, they can get out of the pushchair and run about a bit. Make it easier for you to push, too.' She strapped the little boys firmly into their double pushchair. 'Now, be good, and Auntie Libby might show you some ponies. Don't stay out too long, Libby. It really is raw out and I don't want you all down with colds. Not with Christmas just round the corner.'

'We won't be too long,' Libby promised and steered the unwieldy vehicle through the door. Outside, she shivered; there really was a cold wind and she looked to make sure that both twins had mittens on. The sooner they got up the hill to the gate which led on to the moor, the better, she thought, then they could get out and run around to keep themselves warm.

There was a small group of wild ponies grazing near the gate. They moved off as Libby came through, but the mere sight of them was enough for the twins, who clamoured to be let out of the chair and, once unstrapped, scurried after the animals, chuckling with delight. Libby followed slowly, her mind drifting away as it still did, even though she did her best to stop it. Where was Keir now, she wondered. And what was he doing? She supposed that he and Pia must be married now; the *contessa* wouldn't have wanted any more delay than necessary, and there would have been no reason for Keir to wait either. Perhaps they had left Malta, gone back to Italy. She supposed that Jeremy would write and tell her one day.

Libby wrenched her mind away from Malta, trying to aim her thoughts at her own future. She had given up her job on the magazine, although she was aware that the editor would always be willing to welcome her back and, even if there were no vacancy there, she could find a place on one of the other magazines published by the same house. But did she want to go back to that life? Wouldn't it be better to make a complete change—find a different kind of job somewhere else, abroad even, start absolutely fresh? Only in that way, she thought, would she be able to sweep her mind and emotions clear of Keir—as much as that was possible, anyway.

In any case, she couldn't impose on Claire and Simon much longer. Welcoming though they had been, they must want their house to themselves again. Libby knew that Clair had been grateful for her help with the twins, who were real handfuls at the toddler stage, but really she was able to cope quite well on her own, and had plenty of friends with children of their own who were always ready to help out.

Perhaps she should go and stay with her mother, who had moved into Plymouth to be nearer her own friends; Mrs Marsh had never really liked Dartmoor. But even as the idea crossed her mind, Libby dismissed it. It wasn't fair, she knew, to blame her mother for a perfectly natural reaction to Dr Marsh's death, but she couldn't forget the effect it had had on her, the way she had sent Keir away. If that hadn't happened, she and Keir might—almost certainly *would*—be together now.

The ponies had galloped out of sight now and the two small, duffle-coated figures scampered back to her, wanting the ball that Libby had brought in her coat pocket. She took it out and threw it, and off they ran again. Really, Claire had been very lucky to have twins, she thought, watching them with affection. They might be more work, but they were real companions to each other, playmates who never had to part. If they never found anyone else, they would always have each other. She sighed enviously, then shook herself. Self-pity again! It really was time she took herself in hand.

When she got back to the house, ready for a cup of tea by the log fire that Claire kept burning all day, she had made up her mind that she must do something definite about the future. No more putting it off, she told herself firmly. It was time to start sitting up and taking notice again. She had promised to stay with Claire and Simon until after Christmas but, although they had assured her that she was welcome for as long as she liked after that, she was determined to leave at the beginning of January. *Something* would turn up before then—and, whatever it was, she'd take it. Go where the wind blows, she thought, shivering a little as she stood outside the door folding up the pushchair. Making plans hasn't worked—leave it to fate instead.

The decision seemed to help her and she felt better during the next few days as she got caught up in the whirl of Christmas preparations. Puddings, cakes, mince pies—Claire seemed to be preparing for an army and was glad of Libby's help, either in the kitchen or in keeping the twins amused. At the end of the week, however, with most of the baking done, she looked at her younger sister with a rueful smile.

'Poor Libby! I've been working you to death, and you came here for a rest! Tell you what, you can have the rest of the day off! Isn't that generous of me?'

'Unpaid, of course,' Libby smiled. 'You don't need to worry, Claire, I've enjoyed it. It's been a complete change for me, and that's what I needed. Resting gives me too much time—to think.'

Claire eyed her sister. Libby had said little about what had happened on Malta, apart from the bare facts, but these had been enough to enable Claire to guess the heartache the younger girl had suffered. Libby knew, however, that Claire would never probe. One day, when she was ready, she would tell her the whole story, but until then her secrets were her own.

'Well, why don't you go out for the day?' Claire suggested now. 'It's a nice day for once, and the twins are going to a birthday party this afternoon. Quite honestly I should rather enjoy being quite alone in the house!'

'Oh well, if you put it like that . . .' Smiling, Libby went to fetch her coat. It really was a nice day, she thought, cold but bright. She would enjoy a day on the moor, walking in the crisp air without the hampering presence of a pushchair. And Claire always had liked a certain amount of solitude—something she didn't get much of these days.

She dressed warmly, in slacks and thick pullover, with an anorak on top. Claire had suggested she take the car—it would be nice to have a real day out—and she hesitated for a moment about where to go. She knew in her heart where she wanted to go, but she wasn't at all sure it would be wise. Would it lay her ghosts—or would it resuscitate them?

It seemed that it was beyond her control anyway, for the car turned on to the moor as if driven by some other agency, and she found herself along the road that she had followed with Keir once—in another life, it seemed. Bemused, detached, she watched the miles roll under her wheels, the granite tors rise on either side, the valleys grow deeper as the hills soared higher. And then she was at the top of the last rise, looking down on the river that gleamed in the sunshine, the two rivers that came together to make one—the moor's own river, the Dart, winding its way down to the sea.

Every year the Dart takes a heart. The saying came into her mind unbidden and she knew that it referred really to the danger that the river could present when swollen and swift with rain. But had her own heart ever really been hers, she wondered as she locked the car and walked out of the car park and along the turbulent stream. She had given it to Keir, and he had kept it. And his last memory of her had been just here, by the river, where they had lain together in a hollow filled with scented heather and she had begged him to make love to her . . .

The heather was dead now, dark and crackling under her feet, and the bracken was brown and withered. She walked along the bank, watching the water as it tumbled over the granite rocks, some of them smoothed and glistening from centuries of constant washing, others standing higher, their tops fuzzed with green moss. A dipper fluttered ahead as if teasing her, small and dark like a white-breasted robin, and then disappeared under the water. It popped out a few yards further on and stood on a rock, eyeing her and flirting its jaunty tail. *You* don't have any worries, she thought. You just have to find enough food each day, raise a family each year and nobody demands any more of you. Lucky little bird!

She and Keir had seen a kingfisher along here once, she remembered. They had frozen, hand in hand, watching its brilliant progress along the bank, and had held their breath as it dived into the water and came up with a small fish struggling in its beak. A good omen, they'd thought it. How wrong you could be!

Pia's pregnancy would be obvious now, the child moving inside her. Libby laid her own hand over her stomach, wondering what it must be like to know that a new life was beginning in there. If only it could be her child—hers and Keir's. The longing gripped at her heart and she stopped, sudden tears misting her eyes. It had been a mistake to come here, she told herself fiercely. But she couldn't turn back now.

A hollow opened up at her feet, and she looked down into it. Surely this was where she had lain with Keir . . . It wasn't easy to tell, but she was certain she remembered that rock—and that particular clump of trees on the opposite bank. Almost automatically, she dropped into it and lay down. She had come so far, she might as well complete her memories. Kill or cure, she thought ironically. It would either lay her ghosts or convince her that they would never be laid.

Small white puffs of cloud raced across the blue sky above, but here in the hollow it was sheltered from the breeze and almost warm. Libby lay with her hands behind her head, staring up until she was dizzy, letting her memories wash over her. Perhaps this was the best way after all. She had been fighting them for so long; maybe after this they would give her some peace.

She closed her eyes. It would be so easy to persuade herself that she was here with Keir again; so easy to imagine his body warm against hers, his lips cool on her mouth . . . She parted her lips, turning slightly as if to nestle closer; and when a pair of lips did indeed touch hers, she responded to the fire that scorched along her veins as if she had been expecting it all along.

'Libby . . . Libby . . .' Keir's voice said, rough with desire.

Libby's eyes flew open. The warmth she had imagined was real—the kiss was actually tangible on her lips—the arms that enclosed her were strong and hard, and not the figments of her imagination.

'*Keir!*' she gasped, and the world swam.

'It's all right,' he murmured. 'Don't look so shattered—it really is me, you're not seeing things.' He laid his lips on hers as if to prove it, and Libby found her arms encircling him, her hands moving over his body in a kind of wonder. How *could* he be here? Had she conjured him up through the sheer strength of her longing? Or was it merely a dream, a dream from which she would wake with an even greater sense of loss?

Well, if it were she wanted to stay asleep for as long as possible! A whimper began in her throat as she moved against Keir, her needs welling up in her as she realised that, by whatever means, she was being given another chance. Perhaps only one chance, perhaps only a chance in a dream, but whatever it was she wasn't going to let this one pass, she *couldn't*. Her fingers shook as she fumbled with the fastenings of his shirt under the thick pullover he wore, and Keir drew away slightly with a quickly indrawn breath. He let go of her to find her fingers with his, holding them close against the warmth of his skin.

'Steady, Libby, my sweet,' he whispered. 'I know how you feel, but don't let's rush things. We've got some talking to do, you and I.'

Libby opened her eyes again and looked at him. 'Isn't

it a dream?' she asked dazedly. 'Are you really here?' The breeze touched her for a moment and she shivered, blinking. 'I thought—I thought—'

'I can guess what you thought,' Keir said gravely. 'I shouldn't have come on you suddenly like that—it was too much of a shock for you. But when I saw you here, just as I last remembered you, I couldn't help myself. Yes, Libby, I'm really here. You're touching me—don't I feel real?'

Libby felt his skin warm under her fingers and nodded, her eyes filling with tears. 'You feel real,' she answered. 'But I couldn't believe it—I've missed you so much. I didn't think I'd ever see you again. I thought—I thought I had to live my life without you.'

Keir's arms tightened around her. 'That's what we've got to talk about. Let's sit up—I find you very distracting, lying down!'

He drew Libby up so that she was leaning against him, close to the warm rock that his body made. Something she could always lean on, she thought drowsily, and wondered again if she could be dreaming. But no—there was something very solid about Keir today, something very real about the sky and the crushed grass and the chuckle of the river. This was no dream.

'But what are you doing here?' she asked after a moment. 'Why have you come—and how did you find me?' A thought struck her rather belatedly. 'And what about Pia? Is—is she all right?'

'I haven't pushed her off Ghar-Lapsi cliffs, if that's what you're thinking!' he said grimly. 'Not that I might not have been tempted . . . I'll start at the end, Libby, not the beginning. I came here because Claire told me you'd gone out for the day and I just wondered if there was a chance . . . and because I had to come here anyway. To see this place again, for myself.' His voice was low as he added: 'I couldn't quite believe my eyes when I came to this hollow and found you lying in it—though I'd seen your car in the car park and knew you must be around somewhere.'

'You've seen Claire? You've been to the house?'

'Well, of course, it was the obvious place to go when I found you weren't in London. I knew Claire would know where you were and I only hoped that you might be here in Devon. You could have gone anywhere, but I would have found you, no matter where you'd gone. The world's not big enough to hide you from me, Libby.'

'But—' Libby gazed at him helplessly '—Keir, I don't understand—'

'All right—this time, I'll go back to the beginning. Or to what seemed to me to be the end—that morning when you left Malta. I came to see the plane go, you know. I watched until it was nothing more than a speck in the sky before I could believe you'd left me.'

'I know. I saw you there.'

'And then I went back to the flat. Pia was there—I hadn't told her where I was going, or anything about you. We'd had the father and mother of all rows the night before when I went back—she's a real she-devil, that one.' He let his fingers stray over one cheek. 'Tore at me with her nails—I think she thought I'd find it stimulating! Unfortunately, I've never gone in for that kind of lovemaking, so it didn't work. But she seemed to have made up her mind that she'd won, and for a while I had to believe her. The child made everything different. I couldn't abandon it to the tender mercies of its mother and the best I could think of was that, once it was born, I'd take it away with me. After that, I couldn't see any kind of future—it would have to be left to fate.'

Fate, Libby thought. She had had much the same idea—to leave her future to fate. But if fate had had anything to do with the present situation, it was surely excelling itself and she would never plan anything again!

'So what happened?' she asked. 'Has Pia changed her mind? Isn't she pregnant after all—was it all a lie? Or—' the thought crossed her mind with a kind of horror '—has she lost the baby? Got—rid of it?'

'No, she hasn't done that,' Keir told her, drawing her closer. 'None of those things has happened. But something else has—or, rather, two things did. They were connected—one sparked off the other—but their result was the same.'

'Keir, stop talking in riddles,' Libby begged. 'Tell me straight out.' She caught his eye and stopped as the truth hit her like a blow, knocking the breath from her body as surely as if she'd been punched. '*Keir! It—it is, isn't it? It's true! You've got your memory back!*'

Keir nodded. His eyes were as blue as the singing sky above and as clear as the moorland stream as he caught her to him in a kiss of pure, exuberant joy. 'That's it! You've got it in one! I've remembered everything, Libby—everything. There are no shadows across my mind now, and I can't tell you how incredible it is. Not that most of the memories are particularly happy ones,' he added soberly, 'but at least they're mine, and *I* know what happened to me—I don't have to rely on other people's versions. It's like being handed back a slice of my life I thought had gone for ever.'

'Oh, Keir, that's wonderful,' Libby told him sincerely. 'I'm so glad. But—how did it happen? And how did it affect you and Pia?'

'Which do you want to know first?' he asked teasingly. 'Well, here's the story as it happened. It was about three days after you left—not very long, though it seemed an eternity to me at the time. I was trying to get things sorted out with Pia; she wanted me to go back to Rome for the wedding and as you can imagine the idea of marrying her anywhere horrified me so much that I just didn't want to think about it. Though I knew I'd have to do something soon, because of the baby. Well, we were arguing about that and I was still trying to get some work done, when one morning Jeremy came in with a very funny expression on his face. Said he'd met this man who seemed to be a friend of the *contessa*—Pia, of course—and he'd finally decided to bring him to the flat. He wasn't happy about it, but the fellow had tracked Pia down, knew somehow that she was there, and he was insisting on seeing her.' He paused, and Libby felt her heart skip. 'He showed the man in—and as soon as I saw him, I knew everything.'

'You did? But how?'

'I'll tell you that in a moment. He was an Italian; tall, dark, handsome, the answer to every maiden's prayer. Only this time he was the answer to mine. He was Raffaello Volturno, and in one fell swoop he gave me back my memory and freed me from Pia's clutches.'

'Raffaello Volturno?' Where had she heard that name before? Libby put her fingers to her forehead—and then she knew. Of course! The man who had been at the reception desk of the hotel in Valletta as she checked out. And *that* was why his accent had been familiar—it had been the same as Pia's!

'Who is he?' she asked, and Keir smiled.

'The man who saved my life, no less. He was one of Pia's lovers, Libby. Before I knew her—and afterwards. After we split up.'

He stopped and watched her, waiting for the effect of his words. Their meaning took a few seconds to sink in; then Libby's eyes widened.

'*After you split up?*' she whispered. 'Then—then you

weren't still living with Pia before you left Italy? You weren't in love with her?'

'Never at any time,' he replied vigorously. 'Oh, I was smitten for a time, I have to admit that—Pia can be *very* charming when she likes. And I was lonely—still searching for something I knew in my heart I could only find in one woman.' His arms tightened again. 'I suppose I'd have realised it in the end and come back to see if there was a chance—any chance—for us. But at that time I could still feel the hatred you'd shown when you sent me away after your father's death. I had no way of knowing if that had changed.'

'It changed gradually, I think,' Libby told him. 'I don't know just when—I just knew, one day, that I'd been wrong, that I didn't hate you any more. But I felt sure *you* must hate *me*.'

'What a lot of time we've wasted,' Keir muttered, and he buried his face in her hair.

'It was my fault,' Libby said honestly. 'I let my mother's bitterness influence me. I shouldn't have done that, and I shan't, any more. From now on, I make up my own mind.'

'My fault too. I ought to have understood, and waited, instead of taking off the way I did. I knew I hadn't caused your father's heart attack intentionally—or even carelessly. He *wanted* to tell me that story, Libby, he'd been wanting to for years, but because at first he couldn't talk about it, your mother would never let him. And don't think I'm blaming her—it was a situation she'd never had to deal with, and she had no way of knowing what was the right thing to do. Her biggest fault was in being over-protective, and that's a very understandable reaction, after what they'd both been through.'

Libby was silent, grateful for his insight. With Keir being a novelist and biographer, she supposed that he would naturally have more understanding of human behaviour than most people, but somehow she had never credited him with it.

'Tell me about Pia and Raffaello,' she said at last. 'Why had he come to Malta?'

'To find Pia, of course. They'd been lovers for years, but I gather it was a pretty stormy relationship. In between times, Pia would attach herself to another man, just as she did to me—more to taunt Raffaello than because she was genuinely in love. He was accustomed to it, and generally took off somewhere until she was ready to come back to him. That was when I'd met him, when Pia and I broke up, which was after quite a short time, and he came back to the *palazzo* to claim her.'

'And he's done the same thing again—he came to Malta for her.' Libby frowned. 'But—what about the baby, Keir? Does he know about it? Does he intend to marry Pia himself, and is he willing to take on another man's child? *Your* child?' Anxiety pierced her as she twisted her head to look up into his face. 'Are *you* willing for that to happen?'

Keir smiled down at her and gave her shoulders a comforting squeeze. 'But that doesn't arise, Libby,' he said joyfully. 'Don't you understand—he and Pia were back together before I ever left Rome. The baby *isn't* mine. And as soon as I saw Raffaelo come in through the door, I knew it. I remembered the way Pia had turned to him—and when. That child couldn't possibly have been mine, and if I hadn't lost my wretched memory I'd have known it all along!'

It was as if a mist had been lifted from Libby's eyes. The sun seemed to blaze down on her upturned face; the colours of the grass, the brown bracken, the few remaining bells of heather, were suddenly enriched with light. The murmur of the river became a joyous bubbling, its broken surface sparkling as it splashed against the rocks.

The baby wasn't Keir's! It belonged to another man, a man who evidently felt far more attached to the fickle Pia than Keir ever had. It was as if a giant broom had suddenly swept every obstacle from their path, leaving the way clear and shining.

'Raffaello is clearly tired of Pia's little games and made up his mind that this time she wouldn't escape him,' Keir went on. 'He's been wanting her to marry him all along—God knows why, but they do seem to be very well matched—and he quite deliberately made her pregnant, knowing that she would never bear an illegitimate child. What he didn't bargain for was the chance that she would repay him by conning some other man into thinking he was the father—me. My lost memory was a godsend to her, and she must have been furious when she found you already in residence.'

'Oh, she was.' Libby shivered a little, thinking of the harsh enmity which had sounded in Pia's voice, the hatred that had spoilt the beautiful violet eyes. 'And is she going to marry Raffaello now?'

'She certainly is. In fact—' Keir glanced at his watch '—the ceremony should be taking place at this very moment. Raffaello was determined to take no more chances, and Pia herself was beginning to get anxious—she didn't want to return to Rome for the wedding and then produce a child only a few months later. I'm afraid she's been hoist with her own petard, but I think they'll make out all right. Raffaello isn't the man to stand any nonsense from his wife, whatever she did before, and Pia will probably settled down and become a good, submissive wife.'

'And is that what you want too?' Libby asked cheekily. 'A good, submissive wife?'

Keir's lips twitched as he looked down at her. 'Who

says I want any kind of wife at all?' he asked. 'Maybe what I've been through lately has put me off the whole idea! Or don't you think that's possible?'

'Oh, I should think it's very possible, Libby answered demurely. 'But you obviously need someone to keep you in order—save you from yourself. Just like Pia.' She lifted her face and let her lips trail softly across his. 'Last time we were here we started something we never finished,' she murmured provocatively. 'We've wasted two whole years, Keir—and I've got a sort of superstitious feeling about it. Maybe it brought us bad luck—let's turn back the clock and try again, shall we?'

Keir's eyes darkened as he looked down at her, and she felt a thrill of anticipation go through her. His head blotted out the sky, the corn-gold hair a nimbus around it, and very gently he lowered Libby back to the dry ground. She felt the weight of his body on hers, the tension of desire in his firm lips; then, as her blood sang and her heart kicked into jubilant life, she began to respond to Keir's urgent caresses with all the exultant abandon that had been repressed for so long—too long, too long.

The breeze, stirring the bushes that surrounded their little hollow, the constant rhythm of the hurrying river, the singing of the birds in the trees on the opposite bank, all provided a music whose sweetness could not be surpassed in the world's greatest concert halls; it accompanied their tender, loving exploration, the excitement that drew them on, on, through a steadily mounting crescendo that led them at last to a wild explosive climax that left them both gasping, clinging to each other like survivors of a storm. As indeed we are, Libby thought dazedly as the world slowly stopped spinning and the sky reeling, and she became gradually conscious once more of the earth beneath her, Keir's weight above her and the dry, rustling grasses, the cool murmur of the water.

Keir raised his head and looked down at her, and his eyes were as dazed as hers. He shook his head slowly, as if to clear it, then laid his cheek against hers and whispered: 'That was like nothing I've ever known before, Libby. I thought I'd made love in the past, but now I know I never did. You are my first woman—just as I am your first man.'

'And last,' she breathed into his ear, and they lay silent for a long time.

This was the true beginning of their life together, Libby thought as she watched the racing clouds high above. From this morning, all worries past, they would stand together. No doubt there would be problems—both she and Keir were too strong-minded not to have disputes—but there would be nothing that love could not overcome. Nothing that could match what they had already been through.

She held Keir tightly and wondered what would come next. Back to Malta, she supposed, to finish the book, but not, she hoped, until after Christmas, a family Christmas with Claire, Simon and the twins was just what she and Keir needed, and it would help to heal the rift between Keir and her mother, too. And then—well, wherever Keir's work took him next. Wherever it was, whatever he did, she would be able to work with him. A partner—not, she hoped, a 'submissive wife'!

Whatever happened, they would always have this memory to cherish. A memory that was not, after all, a 'rooted sorrow' but one that would grow and flourish, a strong healthy plant that they would tend with care for the rest of their lives.